KEEP YOU BOTH

KATHRYN NOLAN

Editing by Faith N. Erline
and Jessica Snyder
Cover by Staci Brillhart

ISBN: 979-8-88643-935-9 (ebook)
ISBN: 979-8-88643-936-6 (paperback)

110123

This one's dedicated to big queer love, in all its forms.

And for the disaster bisexuals, of course. Try not to panic!

1

SOMETHING BORROWED

THE FUTURE BRIDE AND GROOM WERE CLEARLY UNHAPPY.

A blustery winter storm approached as we wandered through the cozy ski lodge I'd foolishly assumed was a sure thing. A harsh wind rattled the floor-to-ceiling windows, scattering flurries of snow and almost obscuring the mountains in the distance.

Yet we were safe and warm inside, with fires crackling in stone hearths still draped in garlands. Bouquets of dried holly berries decorated every reading nook and window seat. And the atmosphere was as charming as it was rustic, the kind of place that radiated *wedded bliss.*

But while Beau and Flora wore matching polite smiles, there was a tightness to their movements, a stilted hesitancy, that had my stomach pitching to the ground.

The venue coordinator—Bethanne—was a friendly blur of motion in front of us. She was just as accommodating in person as she'd been on the phone when I'd called earlier this week and begged for a last-minute walk-through. No easy feat, given the extremely short notice and that it was New Year's Eve weekend.

"I hope the three of you had a lovely holiday," she trilled. "How many venues has Paige brought you to visit since you've gotten engaged?"

Flora wrinkled her nose. "It's been so many, it's hard to keep track. Ten, maybe?"

"This will be the seventeenth," I corrected.

Beau's lips twitched as he shrugged his massive shoulders. "I promise we're not usually this picky. Just haven't found a place that feels right yet."

Bethanne leaned in close, like she was about to share a secret. "Trust me, I've seen it all. You're not the first happy couple to find this process bewildering."

Then she beckoned them to follow her, past the gleaming professional kitchen and the wide verandas. I hung back, only half listening to Bethanne's marketing pitch for why booking this ski lodge was *the smartest thing* they could do. Tilting my head, I tried to picture Beau and Flora's wedding day here. My imagination scrambled to sketch in the sensory details: the rosy summer sun heating the room, filled with their friends and family. The dried berries replaced with blushing peonies, the sky a blazing blue against the backdrop of the Rocky Mountains.

I could see it easily because I'd planned a dozen celebrations in cute mountain towns just like Telluride. Had done a wedding for every season and every type of couple.

So the detailed logistics weren't causing my mental glitch.

Bethanne paused in front of a long table, methodically explaining their dinner options for the big day. They angled toward the menu as she spoke, but at least a foot of distance separated them. Flora nodded pleasantly, though her teeth worried at her bottom lip. Beau squeezed the back of his neck—a nervous tic I could spot from a mile away—and my gaze snagged on the tattoos that decorated his fingers, the ink stretching across his forearms to disappear beneath the shirt cuffed at his elbows.

I shifted on my feet, a heady awareness prickling at the same spot on my neck. And when Beau caught me staring, he sent me a wink that made my face burn.

Pay attention, I mouthed as haughtily as I could manage.

His response was a lopsided grin that never ceased to generate the same reaction, every damn time, and growing more substantial by the day: a fluttering like bird's wings in my belly. His green eyes and dark brows were pretty and soulful—the Nice Boy Next Door, here to capture your heart with his sweet romantic gestures.

But there was nothing sweet about his angular jaw *or* that mouth of his. It was pure sin, made sexier by the husky edges of a Southern accent he still carried, even years after moving to Colorado.

"Now how did you two meet?" Bethanne asked, moving us back to the largest stone hearth. Warmth from the fire licked along my calves, the backs of my knees.

Flora arched an eyebrow Beau's way. "A big group of us, Paige included, met a few years ago at a film festival in Boulder, where we live. We were all super close, still are, but Beau and I started spending extra time together. And by our second date, I was an absolute goner for the guy. Still am."

Pink flushed his cheeks. "We both knew right away that we had something special. I fell hard and fast, couldn't wait to marry her. We proposed to each other at the top of the giant Ferris wheel at Elitch Gardens. Flora's was beautiful and sincere while I babbled along like a lovestruck fool."

Bethanne swooned at this while Flora's expression

turned tender. "There was nothing foolish about what you said to me, Beau Duvall."

"Maybe so," he drawled. "I am lovestruck, darlin'. No arguing that."

Bethanne laughed, but I wasn't buying the act. Not their words, but their body language, the odd awkwardness that hung in the conspicuous space between them. An awkwardness that had appeared a couple months ago, though I'd brushed it off as the usual stress around wedding planning. Yet there was no denying their usual flirtatious affection had been replaced by whatever *this* was—some song-and-dance they broke out for every vendor we visited before retreating back to their clumsy tension.

I hadn't seen them so much as hold hands recently. No stolen kisses when they thought I wasn't looking or long, lingering hugs. This from two people who were usually permanently entwined. The conflicting emotions this inspired in me were impossible to untangle. A hope tinged with heartbreak. Relief crushed by disbelief.

We were six agonizing months into this process, and Beau and Flora were no longer the couple they'd been on the morning they'd shared the news of their engagement. I'd spent days working up the courage to finally see them after my year in California—and I'd known within *minutes* that it was a mistake. Made even worse when they told me they'd gotten engaged that weekend. My palms had gone slick at the news, my stomach hollowing with nerves.

Beau, on the other hand, spent the morning enamored, gazing at Flora's profile like he was trying to memorize every stray freckle scattered across the bridge of her nose.

And Flora had been lit from within, as stunning as ever with her honey-blond hair in a messy topknot, smoky eyeliner smudged from sleep, her smile shy. Every time her wide brown eyes had landed on mine, I'd fought the fierce urge to reach for her beneath the table.

I didn't though. Couldn't. My anguish was so familiar to me that I welcomed it like an old friend.

"Well, I should probably leave you three to it, especially with this storm coming in," Bethanne said. "Please continue wandering around, of course. Paige, do you want to step into my office so I can give you all the boring paperwork?"

"Absolutely," I replied, before turning back to the bride and groom. "Try not to get into any trouble."

Beau's grin flashed. "We make no promises."

I shot him a scowl then followed Bethanne down a long hallway. In my workbag, I had a slim binder with Beau's and Flora's names on it—shockingly slim given the timing. No alterations had been scheduled, no photographers booked, not even a save-the-date postcard planned. I'd overseen two weddings and a commitment ceremony in the six months it had taken us to eliminate sixteen other venues.

As Bethanne handed me documents and sample contracts, she said, "Do they have a date in mind? Because we book up so fast, they'll be lucky to find anything for this coming year."

I hesitated. "They're considering the summer, but no exact date yet."

"*This* summer?"

I tacked on a polite smile. "Beau and Flora are having a difficult time narrowing down exactly what they want."

"Interesting. Best of luck to you then, I know how challenging your job can be." She cocked her head toward the hallway. "Lovely couple, though."

My smile froze in place. "Truly."

Back out in the main room, I followed the sound of hushed voices until I found them in a small library. Beau was raking a hand through his hair, brows knit together. Flora's eyes were glued to the floor, shoulders hunched forward. I leaned against the door frame and cleared my throat. They startled, attempting to smooth their anxious expressions. More than a foot separated them. Still.

Every muscle in my body went taut.

"So...what do we think?" I asked carefully. "Do we have ourselves a winner?"

They shared a look too cryptic for me to decipher. With a sigh, Flora crossed the room and slipped into my arms, tucking her head beneath my chin. I wavered, as always. Met Beau's gaze from across the room and saw the fire that burned there. The way his eyes lingered at every place where our bodies touched. It scorched like jealousy but also *desire*, the dual emotions mimicking the ones at the very core of my being. It was in the way his fingers flexed against the top of his thighs. The bob of his throat. The hardening of his jaw.

Flora had scarcely touched Beau in my presence in weeks. That hadn't stopped her from snuggling up to me just like this whenever she could.

One of my hands landed gently between her shoulder blades, while the other cupped the back of her head. My mouth dropped to her hair on pure instinct. The soft inhale that followed was just as instinctual—breathing in her woodsy, lavender scent.

A bolt of pure yearning rushed through me.

Flora exhaled, her breath caressing the hollow of my throat. I allowed my hand to stroke through her hair once —*only* once—before raising my eyes to Beau's again.

Another tick of his jaw. Another deliberate perusal.

"Don't be mad, but this venue isn't the one," Flora said, her voice muffled against my skin.

My stomach roiled with frustration while my heart sang with relief. I reared back to catch her eye, pressing our hips together. This close, she was all thick, dramatic brows and rosy lips with the *tiniest* gap between her two front teeth. A spray of freckles across her nose and the flash of a gold septum piercing.

Adorable. Beautiful. A temptation I clutched tightly in my arms as if her fiancé wasn't right beside us.

"After you passed on the last three, you said you wanted something more rustic and out-of-the-way." I waved my hand to indicate the rustic, out-of-the-way details all around us. "What's not to love? It's got fireplaces and quaint mountain views and antlers on the wall."

Beau lifted a shoulder. "We really wanted to love it, Paige."

Flora shook her head. "Every venue you've shown us has been so wonderful. It's not you, it's definitely us. I don't want you to feel like you're wasting your time."

I raised a brow. "It's not a waste of my time because I'd help you with anything. You know that. But the two of you have always been so—"

"Devastatingly handsome?" Beau offered.

"A pain in my ass," I clarified with a smile. "And also *decisive*. You always know what you want."

He pushed to stand, joining us by the door. "Not this time."

I lowered my voice. "I'm not only here to figure out seating arrangements. We're friends first, always. So if there's...something else going on, some problem that you need to share with me, I'm here to listen."

They avoided eye contact and stayed silent. My heart

stuttered. But then a snow-laden pine tree battered against the window, springing all three of us apart.

Beau whistled under his breath. "This storm's gonna be a bad one. There's no way you can drive back to Boulder in this, Paige. The roads out of Telluride will be closed soon, if they aren't already."

"I'll be fine," I said quickly. "I've driven in worse."

"Why don't you crash with us for the weekend?" Flora asked. "There's an extra bedroom and everything."

A rush of unease raced down my spine. "Uh...what?"

Beau leaned his forearm against the door frame. "The cabin we rented for New Year's isn't far from here, and we packed tons of supplies. It'll be cozy as hell. And you *love* cozy."

"Sure, but I can't...I can't just *impose* on your romantic holiday weekend because of a little bad weather."

A gust of wind shook the windows again, sending the rapidly falling snow into a churning chaos. All three of our phones chimed with a severe weather alert for Telluride, and my screen became filled with phrases like *hazardous conditions* and *advised not to travel* and *residents could lose power*.

"It's not imposing if we're asking you to," Flora said, gazing up at me through her dark lashes. "Besides, you have to help me drink all the champagne that we packed."

"Great point, Flor." Beau's cocky grin had returned. "And I wouldn't even call it *askin'*. We're demanding it, Paige Presley."

Be trapped in a cabin with only Beau and Flora and too much champagne?

No *fucking* way.

All that fizzy sweetness, all those loose limbs and

lowered inhibitions. No extra friends to lighten the tension. No outside world to distract us.

The truth was, I wanted Beau and Flora—wanted them *both*—with a desperation that bordered on obsession.

Except they were engaged to be married.

And I was their wedding planner.

2

MODESTY ISN'T REALLY MY THING

THEIR CABIN WAS BARELY VISIBLE THROUGH THE HAZE OF snow.

The tires crunched as I carefully maneuvered my car down the sloping driveway, parking it behind Beau and Flora's. Warm light spilled from the windows of the cabin like honey tipped from a cup. Through the flurries, the front door was ruby red against the wood. Christmas lights bordered the roof and twinkled, star-like, in the bushes.

The blizzard continued dumping wet clumps of snow, sealing my fate. And the short drive here felt dangerous enough, my hands gripping the wheel so tightly my joints ached. I'd sent a cautious message to our group chat, which included Beau, Flora and the rest of the people we'd become fast friends with after all meeting at the Mile High Horror Film Festival a few years back. We were a tight-knit group of queer weirdos with a shared obsession for scary movies and camping trips. Though Beau, Flora and I had immediately clicked on a deeper level and spent the first part of our friendship virtually inseparable.

Until they started dating, that is.

The weather's pretty nasty here, was thinking of crashing with Beau and Flora, I'd texted. *Unless you all think I can make it back??? I really don't want to miss the New Queers Eve dance party. Already bought my platform shoes!*

Within seconds, Flora had responded: *Telluride is currently experiencing a snowpocalypse. Visibility: zero. Wind chill: fucking freezing. She's staying. Plus, we can have a big gay dance party once we all return...SAFELY!!!*

The rest of the group chimed in and affirmed Flora's explanation, with no understanding of how this situation would affect *me.* Stranded in a cabin, for who knew *how* long, with the two people I wanted the most but could never have. Two people whose wedding I was supposed to be planning in a precise and professional manner, regardless of my feelings for them.

Two people who were *clearly* having problems...but refused to tell me why.

With a heavy sigh, I scanned the responses, which were all some variation of "do you want to *die*?"

I didn't. Though death from unrequited love was a possibility this weekend.

Beau's response came through. *Told ya, Paige. You're stuck with us.*

I released a strangled breath and shot him a glare through the windshield. He managed to look confident and jaunty even in the midst of the snowpocalypse. He knocked on my window, and I reluctantly rolled it down a few inches. Flora appeared by his side, flurries clinging to her golden hair, holding up a house key.

"Come on, Paige," she said. "My plan was to bake all weekend, including gingerbread cake with cream cheese frosting."

My face flushed. "My favorite?"

"Anything for you," she sang. "And if we're snowed in, I'm sure we'll find something to do to pass the time."

That flush turned blistering. My eyes landed on the venue paperwork sticking out of my event binder. "Fine. I'm in. But *only* if we spend that time nailing down where the hell it is that you're getting married. We need to decide." I coughed, shook my head. "*You* need to decide before every spot is taken for the summer."

They exchanged another look, partially obscured by the snow. Flora took a step to the side, putting more space between them. Beau squeezed the back of his neck.

"No deal," he said. "No more wedding details. It's almost New Year's Eve. We're snowbound, and we need to have some fun. No meal counts. No dates. No alterations."

I held his gaze. "Are you fucking with me right now?"

"Not one bit. Flor and I need a break." He gave a short nod, like he was tipping a cowboy hat my way. "Now get your sweet ass inside that cabin."

Then they turned and began picking their way through the snow, overnight luggage and grocery bags in hand. I hinged forward at the waist and rolled the window all the way down. "A break? What does that even...a break from *what*?"

But they either couldn't hear me over the wind...or were blatantly ignoring me. I narrowed my eyes at their retreating backs. This wasn't my first experience with the mercurial whims of clients. My base skewed toward the queer and quirky, but that didn't mean my job was free of drama. Managing expectations was part of the gig.

I didn't anticipate it from Beau and Flora though. Not this frustrating indecisiveness. And not whatever weird awkward energy was swirling around them. It wasn't only because of our close friendship but who they were as a couple. They were both bisexual, like me. Charming and affectionate, laid-back but still adventurous. When they'd asked me to be their wedding planner, I'd imagined a free-spirited backyard BBQ. Wildflower bouquets and an all-night dance party. Something carefree and full of community.

Instead, we'd driven all across the state of Colorado in search of a perfect venue I feared didn't actually exist.

I tugged a beanie down over my chin-length black curls and grabbed my workbag. Within seconds of stepping outside, I knew there was no other option but to stay at the cabin. The snow was falling too fast, and I could barely see my hand in front of my face. Ice stung my cheeks as I attempted the treacherous walk up the front brick path. The soaring Rockies pressed in all around us, and I was dimly aware of a few other houses in the distance.

The ruby-red door swung open, and Beau's big, broad-shouldered frame appeared. "Paige? I'm comin' to get ya."

I snorted. "I'm a Colorado native. Pretty sure I can handle—"

My boot slipped so fast on a patch of ice that my leg flew straight up and I plummeted to the ground. One second I was standing—the next, I was blinking up into a pure white haze. Another blink, and Beau's face appeared. There was a split-second of extreme worry in his eyes before his training kicked in. "Did you take a tumble, gorgeous?"

"As I was *saying*, I'm a Colorado native and can handle myself."

His eyes roamed my face then traveled the length of my body, searching for hidden injuries. "If you're crackin' jokes, you'll live. Trust me, I'm a professional."

"Did they teach you this kind of witty bedside manner at paramedic school?"

He chuckled. "You're adorable when you try to talk shit." His fingers pressed gingerly beneath my hat. "Did you hit your head?"

"No, I caught myself before that happened," I said.

His big hands gripped my cheeks, surprisingly warm in the biting cold. "I'll still assess you inside. What else hurts?"

I wiggled my fingers and toes, wincing when my ankle protested. "Ah, fuck. My left ankle, the one that slipped."

"You probably twisted it, but I can patch you up." He relaxed into a crooked grin. "It's smart to have a devastatingly handsome paramedic on hand if you're trapped in the middle of nowhere."

"Can I request one that's less annoying though?"

He winked. "You love it, Paige Presley. And I'm sorry to say, but you're stuck with me this weekend. So let's see about getting you to stand, okay?"

Still crouching, Beau helped me to sit, then to a very careful standing position. I tried to put weight on my ankle and cursed instead.

"I can't... It hurts too much right now," I blurted out. Snow swirled around us, soaking my hair and sending icy water through my layers.

Beau stepped in front of me, gripping me by the shoulders. He glanced down then back up the walkway. "I'll carry you inside, as long as that's all right with you?"

Heat coursed through me, even in the freezing cold. "Are you sure?"

His answer was to scoop me up into his arms like he'd done it a million times before. The new position brought me tight against his burly chest and inches away from that sinful mouth. Though it was the very real concern in his eyes that awakened the bird-like fluttering in my belly. A concern that soon melted away and became something like curiosity.

Then a smug satisfaction.

"Can I take us inside, or do you need more time to stare at my face?" he asked, his voice low and raspy.

I jerked my chin up in challenge. "I wasn't staring at your face, as much as I know you'd love that. I was only wondering if they taught you how to swoop in and dramatically carry people to safety in paramedic school."

Beau hefted me an inch higher then began to trudge inside. "Wouldn't you like to know."

"Well...you're quite good at it. Is what I was trying to say."

He leveled me with another fiery stare. "I'm quite good at a lot of things."

Once inside, my first impression was of a statuesque Christmas tree in the corner, burgundy throw rugs, armchairs piled high with pillows, a fireplace with a stone hearth, and a retro-looking kitchen. The electric fireplace had already been flicked on, so Beau beelined to the forest-green couch directly next to the flames. He set me down gently before quickly tossing his snow-covered outerwear into the mud room. When he returned, he shoved his sleeves to his forearms and sank to his knees in front of me.

Blood rushed in my ears as Beau lifted a wet curl from my cheek. "I need to see if this place has a first aid kit so I can wrap your ankle. But first, can you follow my finger for me?"

I nodded and did as I was told, warming beneath his professional attention. He tugged off my drenched beanie and sat next to me to examine my head, his fingers sifting through my hair and sending shivers down my neck. "And nothing else hurts, right?"

"Just my ankle."

He grunted his approval and peered deeply into my eyes again. I knew he was only watching my pupils, concerned about a head injury. My heart still danced in my chest the longer that he stared at me.

"You know," he said softly, "I wouldn't have passed any of my exams or certifications to become a paramedic if you and Flora hadn't helped me."

I frowned. "You're the one who aced everything, Beau."

"And I couldn't have done it if you hadn't taken care of me. Fed me food and caffeine, kept me laughing when I wanted to quit. Kept me focused when I felt defeated." His fingers found my chin, holding my face still. "That's not nothin'."

"We would do it again in a heartbeat," I whispered.

His throat worked. "I know you would. It's why I'm so grateful."

Those months were a heady blur of memories, fueled by coffee and catnaps. I had a heavy slate of events to plan, and Flora was just opening up her bakery. All three of us were scrambling to achieve our dreams, flushed with whimsical ambition. Exhaustion hit us after, but in the moment, we were all high on a euphoric adrenaline.

On one of the many nights that we'd been quizzing Beau for his certification at my apartment, I'd woken around four in the morning to find him sprawled asleep on the floor, head in the crook of his elbow. Meanwhile, Flora must have crawled in next to me on the couch. I woke with her head on my chest, our legs intertwined, my lips in her hair. I dragged my fingers through the strands and took long, greedy inhales of her lavender scent. Stared down at her body—her bare thighs draped over mine, the purple nail polish on her toes, the soft press of her breasts against my rib cage.

I had wanted her awake. Wanted her to kiss up the side of my neck while her fingers dipped inside my shorts. Wanted Beau to watch Flora make me come on the couch at four in the morning, so frenzied and sleep-drunk we could convince ourselves it was nothing more than a fever dream in the morning.

Flora appeared in the room as if summoned by my inappropriate thoughts. "What happened? Are you okay?"

"She slipped on the ice and likely twisted an ankle," Beau replied, eyes still on mine. "Do you mind gettin' her out of these wet clothes while I search for a first aid kit?"

Flora vanished then reappeared with clothing that I recognized. "Not at all. Paige, you can borrow whatever you need from me and Beau this weekend. The bathroom was pretty well-stocked. I'd check there first while I take care of our girl."

Flora took Beau's place—kneeling in front of me with a worried expression—while my breath caught in my throat at the mere suggestion of being *their girl*. Even if it was only a joke. Even if it was only their usual affectionate teasing.

There was nothing I yearned for more in this world than for that to be true.

To belong to them both.

"How badly are you hurt?" she asked. "Does Beau think we need to drive you to the hospital?"

I waved away the suggestion. "I'm already feeling better. It's sore but not too bad. With a bit of rest and some whiskey, I'll be good as new tomorrow." I pitched forward to grab at a shoelace. "And I can absolutely undress myself."

Her lips curved up, dark eyes turning playful. "Not on

my watch." She propped my non-injured foot on her thigh and began yanking at the wet laces. "You've spent the past six months taking care of me and Beau nonstop. Let us take care of *you*, Paige."

"Planning your wedding isn't exactly the same as taking care of you," I argued. "It's my job, what I love to do. It...it makes me happy. And it's not every day that a girl gets to plan her best friends' big queer wedding. It's an honor, not a hardship."

The lie sat heavy in my gut. Flora's suddenly cagey expression made it heavier. "I know you want to help. It's why we asked you. Not only because of our friendship but because of how talented you are."

One shoe slid off, and she started on the next foot— gingerly, to avoid hurting me. Her fingers were deft and sure, unlike the growing apprehension in her eyes.

"Flora," I said softly. "There's going to be a wedding...right?"

Her eyes slid to the floor, and she sniffed. Then her fingers pulled at the bottom of my sweater and she clicked her tongue. "This is soaked through, babe. Off it comes."

I settled my fingers over hers, stilling her. "You didn't answer my question."

She cocked her head, her cranberry-colored lips kicking up into a smile. "That's breaking the rules. We said no wedding talk this weekend, remember?"

"*You* said that. I didn't agree."

Another tug of my shirt. A widening of that sweet smile I could never, *ever*, resist. "Sweater. Off. Now. And don't worry, I'll look away."

"Oh, that's not something I care about," I said as she raised the material up and over. "Remember the whole group of us skinny dipping on that camping trip at Echo Lake? Modesty isn't really my thing."

Flora pressed a worn sweatshirt into my hands. It was oversized, with frayed cuffs and faded lettering that read *Rocky Mountain National Park.* A favorite of hers, one she'd worn plenty of late nights when I'd stayed to help her at her bakery.

Now, her pretty gaze lifted to the top of my head instead of traveling down my body. Her front teeth snagged on her bottom lip as she smoothed my mussed hair, tucking strands behind my ear. Pushing errant curls from my forehead, setting off sparks of pleasure that danced across my skin.

"You know what I remember about Echo Lake?" she said, eyes landing back on mine. "That hike you and I went on by ourselves. The one where we—"

"Got completely caught in the pouring rain?" I finished. "We had to hunker under my poncho for an hour until we could make it back down."

Raindrops had glittered in her hair, sliding down her bare thighs. Every time she'd laughed, I'd wanted to drag her into my lap.

Flora sat back on her heels and nodded. "You were so gallant that day. Holding my hand on the tricky parts. Keeping me entertained while we waited out the storm. Helping me leap over the puddles so I wouldn't get wet. I thought you were trying to seduce me."

I huffed out a shocked laugh. "*Seduce* you? What was it, the peanut butter and jelly sandwich I made for our lunch? Or how sweaty and mud-covered I was by the end of it?"

She pushed up on her knees and carefully removed the soft sweatshirt from my clenched fingers. I closed my eyes as she tugged it over my head, and when I opened them again, her face was close to mine. A thrill shot through me as I inhaled the scent of her detergent, amplified when she lowered her voice to a husky whisper.

"Don't pretend you don't know, Paige," she said.

"Know...know what?" I stammered.

"The effect that you have on people," she said, almost a plea. "The effect that you have on me."

I blinked, taken aback. And that's when Beau returned with a first aid kit.

"Let me guess," he said. "Paige is refusing to let us take care of her."

"That she is."

Then Beau dropped to his knees next to Flora and I inhaled a shaky breath.

"I'm not letting you start off New Year's Eve weekend with a busted ankle and hypothermia," he said with a sly grin. "So stop your fussin' and let us take off these pants. They'll turn you into an icicle."

I had no response to that demand. Not when they both placed their hands on my bare ankles with matching looks of reverence on their faces. Not when two sets of eyes found mine, full of a longing that took my breath away. That longing wasn't directed toward each other though—there was a six-inch gap between their bodies, and they hadn't made eye contact once.

"I don't...I don't need you to take care of me," I managed to say.

Beau's gaze darkened. "That wasn't a request, Paige." His strong hands came to my waist. "Now stand up and lean against me. It'll make it easier for Flora."

My lips twisted to the side. "Someone's feeling bossy."

His response was a subtle quirk of his eyebrow. I obeyed, letting myself be pulled into place. His fingers tightened, pressing into my skin while I shifted onto my good ankle. Beau's eyes were locked on mine while Flora's stayed to the side. Though it only made me *more* aware that I was half-naked in front of two people whose hands roamed my body so very carefully. I felt her tug on the waistband of my pants then slowly drag them down my legs. Her breath feathered along my thighs, across my knees. Then back up again as she redressed me in a pair of her old sweatpants.

"Better?" she asked.

"Much."

Beau helped me back down and tenderly set my injured foot on his thigh. The muscle twitched and flexed, reminding me of how strong and thick he was there. The large tattoos that decorated his skin, the dark dusting of hair. He began wrapping my ankle with expert precision, sending shivers up my spine every time his fingertips brushed my skin. Next to me, Flora used a towel to squeeze the snow out of my curls. When she finished, she tousled them affectionately.

My entire body ached with the need to be *closer*—to wrap my arms around Flora's waist. To bring Beau's handsome face to ours. To feel his tattooed hands on my hips. Flora's lips on my neck.

Instead, I murmured, "Are you guys...okay? As a couple, I mean. I'm not imagining that there's something weird going on, right?"

Beau tensed. Flora's fingers stilled in my hair, then slipped away. She moved to stand, putting distance between us. "We're fine, just a little tired," she said, with a distinct edge to her voice. "But I think it's high time I started dinner. My plan was whiskey cocktails, buttery biscuits, and roasted chicken. Whaddya say?"

My stomach grumbled despite the awkward moment.

She cracked a smile, though it didn't quite reach her eyes. "Sounds like a yes to me," she said, spinning on her heel and heading toward the kitchen. "Maybe we could all go in the hot tub after?"

A blush burned its way up my throat. "A...a hot tub? All three of us?"

Beau's thumb caressed the back of my calf. "As long as you're feeling up to it."

"You're the expert medical professional. Is it recommended for a twisted ankle?"

His green eyes twinkled. "It absolutely is. We learned that on day one." Then he helped me rise to my feet before bending and lifting me against his chest again. "How does the ankle feel, by the way?"

I flexed it experimentally. "Perfect. It barely hurts."

He lowered his voice. "Told ya I was good."

Beau was staring at my mouth with a look I could only describe as *ravenous*. He smelled crisp and earthy, like the pine trees outside. And the open vee of his Henley revealed a hint of chest hair and the ink of his tattoos. The fraught tension hanging between all three of us made Flora's hot tub suggestion seem especially dangerous. I wouldn't survive seeing them sweat-slicked and half-naked, simultaneously hyper-focusing on me while ignoring each other.

It was as tempting as it was concerning—this spiky wedge lodged between them. The sudden conflict they refused to acknowledge or talk about. We once told each other everything, every wild dream and feverish secret.

Well, except for one.

From the moment they started dating, I'd tucked my feelings for them deep inside my heart, never to see the light of day. So deep that my need became an incessant and ever-lasting craving, turning me into the worst kind of masochist.

Yes, I'll plan your wedding.

Yes, I'll be there every step of the way.

Yes, I'll spend a weekend trapped in a cabin with you.

So really, what was a little bit of extra pain in the grand scheme of things?

3

A TENDER HEART

Beau carried me effortlessly around the cabin.

Bay windows revealed the wintry squall outside. More than a foot of snow had fallen, and wind continued to shake the pine trees, sending branches whipping through the air. Inside, every room was filled with a rich, rosy light and opulent rugs. Twinkle lights curled over the hearth and up the banisters, as delicate as summer fireflies.

Wooden floors gleamed beneath our feet while buttery baking smells wafted in from the kitchen. Behind us came the bustling sounds of pots and pans, water running and Flora singing as she cooked.

Beau stopped in front of the second bedroom, decked out in colors of teal and white. "Thought this one could be yours," he said. "It has a window seat and everything. Perfect for my favorite bookworm."

My heart leaped at the sight of it. Imagined myself gazing out at a quiet, snowy dawn. The colors of the indigo sky spilling across the snow before the sun rose, turning everything bright and dazzling.

"How did you know I'd love it?" I asked.

"Because I know *you*," he said softly. "Though I hope you don't mind your bedroom being directly next to ours."

"Oh that's...that's whatever. I mean, that's fine," I sputtered. "It's really not a bad place to get snowed in, yeah?"

He arched a brow. "We've done more with less. It's better than that two-bedroom condo we rented for the whole group of us in Denver for Pride that first summer we knew each other."

"You mean when I slept in the fucking *bathtub*?"

Beau moved fully into my bedroom, stopping to place me on the window seat. He sprawled out next to me, letting his knee press into mine. "I'm surprised you remember much of anything, considering you were drunk as hell."

My hand flew to my eyes. "Shit, that's right. Tell me I didn't say or do anything too embarrassing."

The sound of his low laughter had my cheeks turning pink. "You're adorable when you're drunk. Adorable when you're sober too," he drawled.

I broke into a smile. "It's tough being this cute, but someone has to do it."

That Pride had been a rainbow-filled day of celebration and dancing, ending with the whole group of us hopping around from gay bar to gay bar. My clearest memory, the one I returned to far too often, was of being pressed between Beau and Flora's bodies on the dance floor. Blissed out and sweaty, laughing outrageously with our arms in the air. I'd never forgotten the solid heat of them, the way their fingers tangled together as they touched me.

The beads of sweat on Flora's collarbone, Beau's face buried in my hair.

I was lucky that I'd fallen asleep as soon as I'd climbed

into that tub. If I'd stayed awake, I would have begged them to join me. Given my loose tongue and one-too-many shots, I wouldn't have stopped there either. Would have spilled every late-night fantasy like apples from a barrel, offering each like a gift. *Here, take this. Here, take me.*

Beau clicked his tongue and caught one of my curls. His eyes lingered on mine, a crease in his brow. He seemed poised to say something but instead dropped his other hand onto my knee, his thumb stroking lightly up my inner thigh. The soft sounds of Flora in the next room faded away, as did the staccato rapping of the branches against the pane. Guilt surged through me...but the pleasure was more powerful. They dueled inside my body while my brain tried to make sense of what was happening.

Beau's throat worked on a swallow, and whatever he was trying *not* to say had his features twisting up.

I should have moved away. Should have knocked Beau's hand from my leg instead of what I actually did—stared at his fingers on my thigh while a roaring, unruly need snapped beneath my skin. Fine hair coated his forearm, the veins and corded muscles standing out against his tattoos. I knew what those powerful hands did. Rescued people. Saved lives.

His thumb caressed me again, more deliberately this time.

"What are you thinking about over there?" he asked, voice husky.

I hesitated, searching for a witty response that wasn't *your sexy hands*. My attention snagged on the underside of Beau's arm, where a detailed portrait of Ripley from the movie *Alien* was tattooed—gun slung across her chest and Jonesy the cat in her arms.

"The night that you got this," I said.

His jaw flexed. "What about it?"

Too late, I realized I'd revealed a memory that was much too sweet and tender.

"We closed down Pearl Street Pub," I said lightly. "They had to kick us out after two a.m."

His fingers tightened on my knee. We'd sat just like this that night, a couple of months after we'd first met. On two bar stools pulled close, our legs entwined, our postures relaxed as the night wore on. His thumb tracing a steady circle, like he was doing now.

We had a lot in common, mostly our love for horror films and tattoos. And on the night in question, I'd sat beside him as he'd gotten his tribute to the classic movie that he loved. After, we shared drinks at our favorite dive bar until closing time. Talking about our favorite movies, reciting our favorite lines, sharing every behind-the-scenes tidbit we knew. It'd been silly and fun and so very nerdy. And as we'd stumbled outside laughing, I desperately wanted Beau to invite me back to his apartment. Could already anticipate the urgency between us—how he'd shove me back against his door and kiss me breathless. Bend me over the first flat surface we came to, so frantic we wouldn't even take off our clothes.

Instead, Beau had peered at me beneath the streetlight with something like shyness. Then he hailed me a cab and kissed me once on the cheek.

"I had the biggest crush on you that night," Beau said, drawing me back to the present, "and didn't know what to do about it."

My pulse skyrocketed, making me dizzy. "Um...what?"

He shot me a look. "Don't play coy. You *so obviously* wanted to kiss me too."

My mouth dropped open, and I raised my hand to give

him the finger. Laughter rumbled from the depths of his chest.

"You're not...that's not...we were having *fun*," I stammered.

He tipped forward and lowered his voice. "I'm teasing you. You weren't the obvious one, *I* was. The whole world stops and pays attention as soon as you walk into a room. Every single time. I was always captivated by you, especially that night. All the ink. All the piercings. Those killer boots. The confidence." His eyes fell to my mouth, his own quirking up at the sides. "That red lipstick you wear just to torture me."

His hand slid another inch up my thigh. I somehow managed to lift my chin. "I don't wear it just to torture you."

His brow cocked with pure arrogance. "You can pretend all you want, gorgeous. But I wanted to kiss you. Badly. And haven't stopped thinking about it since."

A terrifying realization crashed through me. All their affectionate touches and sweet flirting. Their sudden aversion to touching *each other*, their refusal to talk about the wedding. A tiny voice in the back of my head had worried they might be breaking up. But every time I heard it, my head filled with so many shrill alarms it was impossible to consider.

Were Beau and Flora having issues in their relationship...because of *me?*

The panic multiplied, looping through my body like cars on a racetrack. Wedding planners were supposed to make their clients happy. Especially if your clients were also your *closest friends*. We weren't supposed to spark doubt or invoke apprehension.

We certainly weren't supposed to flirt with them *back*.

And there was no way to neatly categorize what a potential break-up truly meant to me. When it came to Beau and Flora, I was forever frozen in limbo—wanting them both, even when they were together. Wanting them to stay together, even if that meant they stayed forbidden. Beau and Flora returning my romantic feelings was technically a dream come true, but I'd never wanted them to break up and date me *separately*.

I never wanted to choose between them. That decision was futile.

From the kitchen came a chorus of beeps and chimes, then the oven door slammed shut. Footfalls in the hallway, getting closer to the bedroom. My eyes widened before I could help it, body going rigid, but Beau was as easygoing as ever. As Flora neared, he slowly settled back and away from me, *slow* being the operative word. His fingers dragged against my skin, like he was reluctant to let me go. He released the curl he'd trapped, but not before tucking it behind my ear. His knuckles grazed down my neck, and I shivered at the caress.

So when Flora ducked her head inside the door to check on us, the smile I tacked on was weak and confused at the edges.

"How are we doing?" she asked brightly.

"Good. Uh...fine. I'm fine. Need any help in the kitchen?" I managed.

"No help. But you can keep me company if you'd like. Have Beau carry you in, and I'll ply you with hot chocolate and bourbon."

She whisked herself away before I could respond. Then I was being hauled up against Beau's chest and carried in Flora's direction. I hadn't responded to his admission.

Wrapped up in his usual rakish charm, I still recognized the vulnerability that beat there like a tender heart.

But when his eyes slid sideways and caught mine, the burning intensity had vanished. He was whistling under his breath with a carefree expression—though I was achingly aware of every spot where our bodies touched.

4

THIS DELIGHTFUL FLAVOR

IN THE KITCHEN, FLORA POINTED TO A BARSTOOL, AND BEAU placed me there gently. He mentioned jumping in the shower before dinner was ready, but I was too aware of his suddenly stilted tone and the way Flora's back stiffened at the sink. She didn't turn around, merely nodded as she rinsed vegetables for a salad. A fresh wave of guilt and confusion washed over me. But as soon as he left, she turned her head and sent a surreptitious smile my way.

And all I could think about was what she'd said to me by the couch—her dark eyes soft, her fingers in my hair. *You were so gallant that day. I thought you were trying to seduce me.*

Flora Stevens was the kind of person that inspired gallantry. From the first moment we'd met, I'd been seized with the urge to bring her flowers and keep her dry in the rain and make her laugh when she was sad. Watching her now—pink-cheeked and flour-dusted, the sleeves of her sweater pushed up to reveal her whisk tattoo—I was gripped by the same desire. Was seriously contemplating making a bouquet out of whatever odds and ends I could find in the house just to present it to her.

Snow fell in great heaps outside, yet the kitchen stayed warm, filled with the smells of freshly baking bread and a chicken roasting in the oven. Beneath Flora's music, I could hear the fire in the hearth, the slight howl of the wind. Mixing bowls and ingredients cluttered the counters, the sight of cheery cooking chaos as intimate to who Flora was as her fingerprint.

She owned a hip and cozy bakery in North Boulder, with lines that stretched down the block during the weekends. Beau and I had spent many a late night and early morning there with her, letting her test recipes on us.

Now she set the tomatoes on a plate to dry and scooped up a large silver mixing bowl. She twirled my way, stepping to stand between my legs.

"I cheated a little bit," she said, and my heart toppled over at her phrasing.

"You...what?" I asked.

She held up a spoon from the bowl, wearing that same covert smile. The one that said *we share a secret*. "I baked the gingerbread cake ahead of time, so all I had to do was whip up the cream cheese frosting. Wanna lick?"

As if I could deny Flora anything.

I wrapped my fingers around hers and brought the spoon to my mouth. Her eyes were bright as I tasted a dollop—butter and molasses and the rich tang of the cheese. She knew this was my favorite recipe of hers and would often sneak slices over to my apartment when I was stressed about a wedding or an event.

I hummed my delight. "Perfect, as always."

She licked frosting from the edge of her palm. "You think so?"

"Of course." I squeezed my thighs together, trapping her where she stood. It was purely instinctual, a yearning to

32

keep her close, but the heat that flared in her eyes kept my knees tight against her hips. "And I'm practically an expert on your recipes at this point. I speak with authority on the matter."

Flora tipped her head, gaze falling to her toes, and I didn't miss the way the pink on her cheeks deepened. "Hearing that you like something I've made still gives me this…this little thrill. I don't know. Is that weird to say?"

"No, not at all," I said, relaxing into a smile. "Why do you think I agreed to plan your wedding? I'm so obviously seeking your compliments, even after all these years."

Her eyes rose back to mine, one hand landing on my knee. Right where Beau had gripped me. I briefly imagined two sets of hands on my body—wandering, stroking, squeezing—and sucked in a breath.

"You're very sweet," she murmured. Her hand came up to grasp my chin. "And you have frosting all over this gorgeous face."

"I like to think it enhances my natural beauty," I said.

Her thumb swiped along my lower lip. She brought it to her mouth and sucked. "You taste delicious, by the way."

"I can't take credit. That's your creation." Then I swiped another dollop of frosting onto my finger and aimed for her cheek. She was too fast, anticipating my move and catching my wrist. Flora brought my finger to her mouth instead, her tongue darting out and curling against my skin.

She sighed approvingly. "I disagree. This delightful flavor is all *you*, Paige Presley."

Whatever laughter had been gathering in my throat died immediately.

"Now who's doing the seducing?" My voice shook slightly.

A wicked grin flew across Flora's face. "What can I say? I'm just a humble, bisexual baker, vying for your affections."

"You've got them," I said, before I could stop myself.

The words seemed to still her, stripping the playfulness from her expression and replacing it with ardent longing. Her gaze raked the length of my body, so different from earlier when I'd been semi-naked with her kneeling in front of me. My brain kept circling around the feel of her tongue, how artfully she'd licked frosting from me. I wondered— with that same burst of guilt tangled with desire—if she would fall to her knees now. Shove my legs open wide and bury her pretty face between them.

Flora blinked and shook her head. She brushed a curl from my forehead and then spun back to the oven, oblivious to the disappointment roaring through me. She ladled something delicious-smelling into a mug and pressed it, steaming, into my hands. Then she grabbed a nearby whiskey bottle and tipped it at the rim, splashing some into the hot chocolate. From the smell alone, I could tell it was her own recipe, the one she sold at the bakery—cocoa with a spoonful of caramel and a pinch of cayenne pepper.

As soon as I sipped it, a languid pleasure unwound through my limbs—the bite of whiskey, the buttery caramel, the spicy heat on my tongue.

It was so good it *almost* made me forget my disappointment.

Almost.

"How's that?" she asked.

"Also perfect."

She hid a smile, turning back to the salad. "Can I ask you something about the wedding?"

"Sure you can," I said, surprised. "I know finding a venue's been tough, but we could start looking at what you want to wear. Oh also, before I forget, do you have a photographer in mind? They do get booked up fast, but I'm sure I could finagle someone last minute."

Her hand moved up and down as she sliced tomatoes and tossed them on top of a bed of lettuce. "No, not...I don't want to talk about all that. I wanted to ask, with the clients you've seen since you started, have any of them ever admitted having...regrets?"

Her back was facing me, head down while she chopped, but the slight cock of her ear told me how intensely she was listening for the answer. Though it was better she hadn't been looking my way. I could feel the shock etched into my face, my fingers trembling when I set down my mug.

"Regret it?" I asked. "Like...later realized they shouldn't have gotten married?"

"Yeah, that. I was curious, is all."

I swallowed hard around a lump in my throat. "Not really. Or at least, not that they've told me. I'm sure over the course of my career at least *one* of the couples will break up. Probably more. And I can guarantee many of them had regrets or fears before and after. Weddings are messy because humans are messy, and that includes all the complicated feelings that come along with it. But I only take clients like us. Queer and trans folks claiming joy as their birthright, declaring a love we've been told we don't deserve."

I hesitated. "It doesn't...doesn't mean all the planning and details and interpersonal stress doesn't take a toll. You and Beau aren't the first couple I've worked with to feel...*stuck* in the process, no matter how festive."

Flora nodded but didn't respond at first. I watched her prepare the salad and place the bowl in the center of the table. Next to it, the roasted chicken and a plate full of fluffy biscuits. When she turned and stepped back between my legs, her expression was difficult to read. Part flirtation, part apprehension. This time, both hands landed above my knees and slid slowly up, tightening mid-thigh. Arousal pulsed through me, warring with my confusion and worries.

"I have a regret," she said simply. "Do you remember that weekend we went dancing together?"

I lifted an eyebrow. "Which one? We're always dancing together."

"The night in the bathroom."

I knew which night she'd meant. Was only playing coy because I didn't want to reveal how often I thought about it, revisiting every moment the same way I did my memories with Beau. Examining every angle. Scrutinizing every touch, every smile. On the night in question, we'd gone somewhere dark and close. Intimate. We'd done shots but not too many, so I remembered every detail. Flora's hands on my hips as we moved together on the dance floor. Our fingers entwined as we sat at the bar. The two of us laughing in the bathroom as I reapplied my lipstick.

Flora had held me from behind as I layered on fresh color. She'd kissed my cheek—a friendly gesture. Affectionate. But then her lips had moved to the nape of my neck, hovering there like she was breathing me in. Then the side of my throat, each kiss sure and confident. Her eyes had met mine in the mirror—smudged eyeliner, glitter on her cheeks, hair wild around her beautiful face.

She'd splayed a hand across my stomach, already coasting lower.

Then lower still.

I'd watched, stunned and barely breathing, as her hand came within inches of cupping my pussy through my jeans. And who knew *what* might have happened next if a trio of sloppy drunk girls hadn't tumbled into the bathroom, shattering our moment like a sledgehammer.

Flora dipped her head close so her mouth was over my ear. My eyes fluttered closed. "You were stunning that night. Everyone in the club wanted you, and you were oblivious. And I had a chance to *kiss you* and didn't. But I dream about it all the time."

It was so similar to Beau's own charged confession that my head spun. I'd wanted them for so long that hearing their whispered honesty—that they'd yearned for me the way I had for them—felt like a thousand Christmas mornings rolled into one.

But I hadn't wanted it like *this*—in the middle of planning their wedding, amid what seemed like a relationship crisis, forcing me back to those unthinkable crossroads.

I didn't want *only* Beau or *only* Flora.

I wanted to keep them both—forever.

5

YOUNG, HOT AND QUEER

FLORA STEPPED AWAY TO CONTINUE PLATING OUR DINNER, leaving me trembling from head to toe on the kitchen counter.

I hadn't replied to what she'd admitted, but she didn't seem to expect it. Simply went about setting an intimate scene for the three of us. She lit candles on the table, dimmed the lights, and placed our utensils with such fondness it tightened my throat.

"What do you think, babe?" she asked, hands on her hips. "Does this work for a New Year's Eve-*Eve* dinner?"

I chewed on my bottom lip. "Flor, can we talk..."

Beau strolled into the kitchen at that exact moment, trapping all the air in my chest. His post-shower hair was still wet and curling at the nape. He paused to finish rolling his sleeves to his elbows, and I noted his flushed cheeks. He smelled like hot steam and the dark woods, alluring and dangerous in equal measure.

Our eyes connected from across the room and his lips curved up, revealing a lazy grin. "I'll be damned. You sure do *look* like Flora followed through on her promise."

"What promise?" I croaked out.

He closed the distance between us and stroked my cheek with the back of his knuckle. "To ply you with hot chocolate and whiskey. Bourbon makes you blush."

His confident hands landed on my waist, gripping me tight before lifting me from the stool then placing me on the floor.

My fingers flew to my face, feeling the traitorous heat there. "Wait, it does?"

Beau pulled out a chair at the table and helped me into it. "Why do you think you're so adorable when you're drunk?"

I managed to sit semi-normally, a major feat given how distracted I was by the tattooed paramedic standing behind me. "Oh, I don't know. I assumed that four to five drinks only improved upon my clever wit and impeccable comedic timing."

He reclined in the chair next to me, raising his own glass of amber liquor. "That's always been true, Paige. But that whiskey blush of yours is awfully pretty."

"I've always thought so," Flora added.

That pretty blush was currently spreading across every square inch of my body. So much so that I longed to tug at my collar, to place an ice cube along my throat and soothe the fire. Flora and Beau exchanged the most fleeting of smiles—there one second, gone the next—and the sight of it did strange things to my nervous system. I was both more confused *and* more relieved. The absence of their easy affection was like the sudden loss of the sun.

I ached for it, even as it burned me.

I cleared my throat, lifted my glass. "I want to say thank you. Not only for laying on the sweetest compliments, and bandaging up my ankle, and cooking my favorite food. But for letting me crash your romantic New Year's Eve plans. It really...it means a lot to me. The two of you always have."

We clinked our glasses together, and suddenly I had two sets of eyes, hot and eager on my face. For a moment, I contemplated begging them *again* to tell me what was really going on. But I hesitated, remembering their swift dismissal every other time.

And let my own cowardice take over, wanting to maintain this tentative truce, no matter how brief.

"It's not crashing if we want you here," Flora said.

Beau tipped his head my way. "And we do want you here. Very, very much."

We sipped together, the only sound the clink of ice cubes on glass. Their twin gazes never left mine though, making it difficult to swallow. We had a gorgeous meal laid out in front of us, yet I was the one being devoured. The intensity grew until I buckled beneath their attention, setting my whiskey down and feigning fascination with the chicken on my plate.

Beau cleared his throat. "All of this looks amazing as usual, Flor."

The first bite of biscuit all but melted in my mouth, and I moaned my agreement. "We don't deserve you."

"Oh, you absolutely do," she said. "Plus, New Year's Eve is my favorite holiday. I'll always go all out, even if the party is three friends snowbound in a cabin together. I *might* have packed sashes and sparklers and hats for tomorrow night." A playful shrug. "And a couple of disco balls to hang."

"You packed all of that for only the two of you?" I asked.

She licked butter from the tip of her thumb. "It's a holiday *just* for wild and unbridled celebration. So we're going to do that, sparklers and all."

"Are we celebrating anything specific?" I asked. "Like, perhaps...your upcoming nuptials?"

Dual shadows darkened their faces—but only for a moment. Flora dropped her chin in her hand and sent me the loveliest smile. "We're celebrating being *alive*. And also being young and hot and queer. Need I say more?"

"No, ma'am," I said with a laugh. "I'm always happy to be my young, hot, queer self."

"This is the holiday of radical change and transformation," she continued. "Saying goodbye to an old year. Welcoming in something new and enchanting. It's intoxicating, all that possibility. Don't you think?"

There was a sharp pang in my chest, the memories of my year in California rising to the surface. Once Beau and Flora started dating, I'd fled to San Francisco with my bruised and wounded heart in tow. It was easy enough to explain away. With my new wedding planning business, I needed to be in a busy market. Besides, Dorothy was there—my best friend from college and the person who would understand why I'd run from their relationship in the first place.

And in the beginning, I'd been captivated by that very same notion. The heady sway of new possibilities. *Maybe I can forget them. Maybe I can let them go.*

In the end, it hadn't been that simple.

In the end, all I did was trade my damaged heart for emotional betrayal. Then stumble back home to Boulder and discover Beau and Flora had gotten engaged.

"It is intoxicating," I finally said. "Scary too, all that potential for change. Sometimes it's easier to stay the course. Safer. Though that would make for a very boring holiday. Less glitter, more apathy."

Beau glanced up from his plate, warmth in his green eyes. "You're one to talk. Starting your business all on your own. Moving to California to have an adventure. Then coming back to Boulder and having even *more* clients? You're like the mascot for radical change."

I was already shaking my head. "I lost a lot of momentum, leaving when I did. I'm lucky for those clients but I burned some bridges I shouldn't have. And I didn't exactly come home for a victory lap. It was more like slinking back home with my head down. I was so embarrassed. After everything that happened with Em and Dorothy when I was in San Francisco..."

Beau's fingers tightened on his glass. Flora's nostrils flared.

"Chasing my dreams with reckless abandon doesn't feel as...as accessible as it used to be," I finished, my throat like a vise.

Flora reached for my hand, caressing my knuckles with her thumb. Beau stood from his chair and grabbed the bottle of bourbon, topping off Flora's glass and then mine. He angled his body forward and poured, close enough that his shoulder pressed against my own.

"What they did was inexcusable in every single way," he said, his Southern accent rough around the edges. "And they clearly had no idea what they were losing when they left you."

I shivered at the rasp in his voice. Then his hand closed around the back of my neck, giving me a squeeze. A gesture I could have written off as friendly if it weren't for the possessiveness in his grip. Flora's thumb faltered on the back of my knuckles.

Faltered, then became a teasing stroke along the side of my wrist. My entire body wanted to melt beneath their combined touch and shared concern. I fought the urge to squirm as a sudden fantasy swept into my thoughts. Food and drinks crashing to the floor as I'm hauled up onto the table and forced to lay back, arms pinned and legs spread. Consumed and enjoyed by their hot mouths and talented fingers, my back arching in pleasure again and again.

In reality, their hands left me at the same time, but with a reluctance that made my chest ache.

"I'm serious, Paige," Beau continued, sinking back into his chair. "You have nothin' to be embarrassed about. Not a damn thing."

"They should be the ones who feel embarrassed. Sounds like they had the opportunity to do the right thing a dozen different times, but in the end, they took the cowardly way out," Flora added. "You deserve so much better than that."

I shot them a grateful look. "I know I do, I just *hate* how much of a stereotype they made me feel. I'm the wedding planner whose girlfriend left her for her *best friend*. It sounds so pathetic. It made me *feel* pathetic."

I paused, tracing the rim of my glass. "I wanted this career because I believe in the radical power of queer love and its many shapes. Romantic love, platonic love, the love of our community and found families. I wanted to be part of something so at odds with our society's rigid rules, spurious as they are. And I still do, obviously. But Em leaving me for Dorothy shook me up in a way I can't entirely explain. It's like I'm...like I'm *skittish* when before I was only ever hopeful. Does that make sense?"

Flora sat back, fiddling with her utensils. "I was infatuated with my first girlfriend. We were in college, and every emotion and feeling felt dialed all the way up. I was twenty years old and ready to marry her then and there. So when she broke up with me, right before graduation, I thought my life was over. I was absolutely inconsolable. I found my way through it, of course. Found my way to other people who treated my heart with more care and kindness. But I know exactly what you mean, Paige. It's devastating."

Beau was nodding, twisting his whiskey in a slow circle. "I had this boyfriend before I met either of you. I was head over heels for the guy and real stupid about it. Had all these dreams of our life together. Wanted him to move in, pretty quickly, but he was always dodging the question. Looking back on it, he was keeping me at arm's length for a reason, but it only made me try harder to keep his attention."

His gaze slid to the side, then locked on mine. "He was cheating on me and had been from the beginning. I found them together, in his apartment. It fucked me up for a long, long time and made it harder to trust, that's for sure."

A spasm of unease bloomed behind my sternum. Not only for my friends' heartbreaks, but because of the truth buried beneath my words. My relationship with Em *did* make me feel skittish—but so had my thwarted longing for the gorgeous couple sitting in front of me. Em leaving me for Dorothy had cracked my heart, but it broke clear in half the day that Beau and Flora shared their engagement.

"They leave a mark," I said, "all these past relationships, all these past friendships. Sometimes for the better, sometimes for the worse. When I try to picture either of you being hurt like that..." I shuddered. "Well, I guess I understand why talking about Em makes you so angry. I'd do anything to go back in time and, I don't know, make them treat you better? Never leave you in the first place?"

Flora gave me a dreamy smile, dropping her chin in her hand. "But then we wouldn't be here together. And I wouldn't change that for the world. I learned a lot from that first experience—about standing up for myself, about my own maturity and all the ways I had room to grow. Ultimately, I discovered that our love is infinite. It doesn't dry up and stop with the first person to break our heart."

"I learned about being truly wanted," Beau said. "I was always chasing his love, chasing his attention. It should have sent up a million red flags, but I only doubled down and tried harder. After, I realized I wanted to be with someone who wanted me as much as I wanted them. No more begging for crumbs."

I bit the end of my thumb, attempting to restrain the many truths crowding the back of my throat. Something like *I learned that throwing myself into a relationship did jack shit to erase my unrequited feelings for the both of you.* Finally, I said, "I'm not quite sure what Em and Dorothy taught me yet. Got any ideas?"

Flora's smile turned wry. "That's up to you, babe. *But* if it helps, Beau and I learned that we're miserable when you're not around us."

I scoffed, suddenly light-headed. "Miserable? No way. You were blissed-out and newly engaged the first time I saw you again."

Beau stood, piling our now empty plates onto his hand. His cocky half-grin felt much too dangerous. "Well, yeah. We were ecstatic that weekend. But Flor's right. It was a long year and we missed you like hell. Even contemplated going out to San Francisco for a surprise visit once or twice, but we talked ourselves out of it every time."

Butterflies multiplied in my stomach—it was Beau's casual flirting and Flora's foot, nudged against mine.

"Why didn't you?" I asked.

He shrugged his broad shoulders but avoided my eyes. Flora stood too, sweeping up the remaining plates, leaving me alone at the table. I frowned, sensing another disturbance between them, and it plunged me right back into the swirling waves of my confusion.

"I would have...would have loved to see you if you had," I said tentatively. "So why did you talk yourselves out of it?"

They shared a longer look this time, something brooding and desperate hanging in the air. Flora's eyes rose to mine and my heart jammed to a stop. "You really want to know?"

"Sure I do," I said, attempting a nonchalance I did *not* feel.

A muscle in Beau's jaw bunched. "We were worried seeing you with Em would make us feel too fucking jealous. And given how we've felt about what she did to you, I'd say we were right."

Beau turned and began washing the dishes while Flora handled the leftovers. Neither gave any indication of the incredible weight of what they'd admitted to me. Nor did they react to my wide eyes and stunned silence.

This day had been one mixed signal after another—an engagement in some kind of peril, their whispered confessions and charged secrets. Every stray caress and lingering glance beckoning me to commit an act no less a betrayal than what Em and Dorothy had done to me.

But if wanting them was wrong, why did every single second I spent in their presence feel so unbelievably right?

6

FULL BOWIE

Half an hour later, I was limping my way toward the hot tub, using the wall for support. We'd dimmed the overhead lights in the cabin, giving everything a wintry glow, and the Christmas tree gleamed with stars and baubles. Beau had sent us from the table with strict instructions to let him tackle the dishes. I'd obeyed in a daze, my thoughts still in total chaos.

We were worried seeing you with Em would make us feel too fucking jealous.

When Flora stared pointedly at my ankle and offered to remove the wrap, I'd shooed her away with the last scraps of my willpower. I wouldn't survive the intimacy, was already deeply concerned about what might happen to me when I joined them in the hot tub. If they would continue to lavish me with attention and affection despite their own awkwardness, sending my mind racing to a dozen different scenarios, each one more devastating than the last.

I made it to the door leading to the hot tub and hesitated at the sight of Flora and Beau, clearly in the middle of a whispered conversation. I couldn't make out their words beneath the sound of the bubbles, but Beau was rubbing the back of his neck. Flora's eyebrows were pinched, her hands gesturing as she spoke. There was a nervous energy to their movements, so at odds with the luxurious surroundings.

From what I could see, the indoor hot tub sat in the middle of a decadent room. Rustic wall sconces gave off an amber-hued lighting, and candle flames flickered in the reflections of the windows. The mountains were no longer visible against the inky-black sky though the storm still raged outside.

Whatever their conversation was about, it was distracting enough that they didn't notice me, hovering in the hallway. Which was good. It gave me time to take in the sight of them in their bathing suits, all that skin exposed and glistening. We'd seen each other—and our friends— half-naked plenty of times, not including the aforementioned skinny dipping in Echo Lake. But I'd always kept my gaze clinical, practically impersonal, a trivial attempt at strengthening my resistance.

Now I stared openly at the delicious curve of Flora's hips in her black bikini bottoms, the intricate tattoos decorating her ribcage. The strands of hair that clung to the nape of her neck, the shape of her breasts beneath her top.

Next to her, Beau was clad in red swim trunks, hair mussed, a shadow of stubble on his jaw. His muscular shoulders were covered in swirling black ink that also spread across his chest, covered in fine dark hair. His thick thighs were on full display, as was the Sailor Jerry-esque pirate ship tattooed on the right one.

I'd caught a glimpse of them once, kissing in an alley as a group of us left our favorite bar. Beau had wrapped Flora's ponytail around his wrist and was tugging her head back, his mouth slanted over hers. She'd hitched her leg high around his waist and his fingers were sliding beneath her skirt. She'd clung to his shoulders, her mouth meeting his over and over, their movements rippling with urgency.

It was brazenly clear to me then. They'd chosen each other, despite the many times they could have chosen *me*.

I'd moved to California shortly after, the image of their bodies fused together burned into my brain.

Beau noticed me first, one eyebrow arching before his lips curved into a grin. My suit was a shirt of his that grazed mid-thigh and his obvious appreciation had my knees going weak. Flora followed his gaze and touched her bottom lip. Her skin was rosy, the rising steam giving her an ethereal look.

"This hot tub is why we booked the place," she said. "What do you think?"

I stepped fully into the room and curled my toes against the cool tile. "Getting snowed in here was a fabulous idea."

She beamed at me, sending my heart skipping. Then she climbed the stairs and descended into the bubbling water looking like a bikini-clad goddess. Beau closed the distance between us and scooped me up into his arms. The rush of body heat from his bare skin was practically indulgent, as was the fluttering of his pulse in the hollow of his throat.

"I know I was putting up a fight before, but a girl could get used to this," I said, sighing as he lowered me into the hot water. The position brought my nose against his hair and his mouth close to my breasts. When he exhaled, I felt it along my collarbone.

"It's a pleasure to serve," he murmured. He released me to the bubbles, and I sank, grateful, into the luxurious steam.

Every single muscle in my body relaxed, even as I was keenly aware that Beau's now-drenched shirt clung to my breasts. The sports bra I'd borrowed from Flora did nothing to stop my nipples from hardening beneath the slick fabric, sending a thrill of sensation down my spine. I ran wet hands through my curls and stretched my neck, opening my eyes to find Beau and Flora openly staring. Admiring me with barely concealed hunger, so fervent I felt drunk on it.

They sat on the same bench, facing me, with a noticeable three feet of separation between them. Beau's arm was draped across the ledge, and a bead of sweat slid down the curve of his bicep. Flora's nipples pebbled beneath her black suit, and my mouth went dry.

I wanted to float between their bodies, yank Flora's suit off and taste her. Wanted Beau's lips on the back of my neck, the space between my shoulder blades. It was the seductive lure of this cabin, isolated in the woods, surrounded by mountains, keeping us safe from the storm. There were no neighbors, no friends, no watchful eyes making me feel guiltier than I already did.

I wasn't going to break up their engagement. I couldn't. *Wouldn't.*

But this obsession had me by the fucking throat. It stole every last bit of air whether I wanted it to or not.

I wrenched my eyes from theirs, shattering the moment.

"Are you bummed you're missing our annual New Queers Eve dance party?" Flora asked, breaking the silence. "I'm sure we'll be getting pictures and videos nonstop tomorrow night."

I pinched my thumb and forefinger together. "A little. You should have seen my outfit. I was going full Bowie. Lightning bolt face paint, silver bell-bottoms, white boots. A fully sequined blazer. Truly, you're missing out on an epic look."

"You would have had every single person in that bar

eating from the palm of your hand," Beau said, lips twitching into a grin. "Who were you planning on kissing at midnight?"

My eyebrows rose. "Kissing? No one. Besides all our drunk friends. I haven't been interested in anyone since I've moved back."

"No one?" Flora asked lightly, but Beau's fingers flexed against the ledge.

"Too busy," I lied. "Weddings don't plan themselves. And like I was saying earlier, it's been hard to put myself back out there when I know all the terrible ways it can go wrong."

Even harder when all you really want is the couple whose wedding you're supposed to be planning.

Hurt creased Flora's face, and Beau's forehead bunched, both reactions surprising me.

"I'm sorry we never came out to see you," Beau said. "Hell, I wish we'd been there when everything went down. I hate knowing you were out there in California, all alone with a broken heart."

I went still in the water. "I'm not sure what you could have done. She was going to leave me for my best friend regardless."

"Been there when you needed us," Flora said. "Kept you company while you fell apart. We could have fed you cookies and wrapped you in blankets and forced you to watch reality television until you finally laughed."

God, how I wanted that now. Though if they'd done that in those early days after my breakup with Em, I would have been far too vulnerable to keep up my usual barriers.

"I would have liked that a lot," I admitted. "I don't... I'm not sure I ever truly loved Em. I was infatuated with her though, and she was super romantic, always coming up with these tiny gestures to make me smile. It was easy to lose myself in her spontaneity, in her grand adventures and future plans. Dorothy was always around then, because I wanted my girlfriend and my college best friend to get along. Obviously they did that a little too well," I said with a humorless laugh.

"Dorothy and I were always falling for the same girls at school, I should have…" I swallowed hard, trying to open my throat. "Should have known better."

Beau's eyes were kind when they met mine. "You miss Dorothy, don't you?"

The answer slammed into me with the same ferocity as the storm outside. "Yes, yes, I miss her more than Em, to be honest. We were *inseparable* in college. She was like my sister and the betrayal was like losing a friend and a sibling, all at once. They kept their affair a secret for months. Let me walk around like an idiot while they were plotting their escape."

The day they finally came clean was fuzzy at best, my brain trying to protect me from the giant rip in my reality caused by the words *We feel terrible, Paige, we really do. But we're in love with each other and there's nothing we can do about it.* Followed by Dorothy driving away with my girl-friend and her things. The image had caused such a stark cognitive dissonance I thought I was in the middle of a nightmare.

"We never spoke again," I added. "They abandoned me so easily, like I was an old pair of shoes that no longer fit. I felt worthless. Completely expendable."

Flora moved through the water and wrapped her arms around my neck. This time, I didn't hesitate to hold her back, noting all the ways her body notched perfectly into mine. "No wonder you feel skittish," she said softly against my cheek. "I'm so sorry, Paige. You deserve the world, and they treated you like shit."

"I'm really okay," I said with a laugh. "I promise. It's just the kind of thing that lingers in the back of my thoughts."

Flora reared back, catching my eye. In that moment, I would have given absolutely anything to kiss her. "Don't give them too much power, okay? They don't deserve the privilege."

Ripples in the water drew my attention to Beau, sliding next to us. Flora's legs tangled with mine, our hips connected below the bubbles. Beau brushed a few curls from my forehead, and his fingers scratched across my scalp. The combined sensations of them touching me, soothing me, was enough to turn my breathing shallow and erratic.

"They really don't deserve it," he drawled. "Want me and Flor to find them and make their life a living hell? Say the word and we'll do it."

I laughed again. "Thank you, but no. I'm sure they're happy together. It was probably for the best, even though the way they went about it was so hurtful. I wasn't the greatest girlfriend to Em. I was easily distracted, not super engaged the last few months. I think I was ready for it to be over, to come back to Boulder, and hadn't realized it yet."

"So what you're saying is, you missed us too much," he said with a wink.

I rolled my eyes. "I missed a lot of people. Not only you two. I'm sure it pains you to accept that I have *other* friends."

Flora tightened her hold on me, pressing her face into my neck. "Don't lie. We're your *favorite* friends."

"Favorite? No way. Third favorite, *maybe*. More like fifth or sixth."

Beau nudged his knuckle beneath my chin. "It's so cute when you try to be a hard-ass. But it never lasts for long."

I made a valiant attempt at fighting a smile but lost when he aimed his own lazy grin in my direction. Flora's fingers trailed down my back, setting off sparks. For a dazzling second, my world clicked into place, floating between the two of them, feeling adored and protected. Just a taste, and I wanted more so badly that an icy fear surged through me.

Fear of ruining what we had, no matter how imperfect. Fear of being the person who meddled with their happiness, the way Dorothy had meddled with mine.

And the worst fear of all—that I was nothing more than a curiosity to them both, a curiosity they could set aside as quickly as Em had.

My heart wouldn't survive being abandoned again.

That same awkward tension surfaced between us, probably brought on by my suddenly rigid muscles and guarded expression. Flora moved away from me, casting a sideways glance at Beau.

Clearing my throat, I made my way toward the steps and grabbed the handles to hoist myself up. "I'm gonna call it a night, actually. It's been a long day and this whole setup is super romantic. It's fucking *snowing* out, and you should get to enjoy the reason why you booked this place." Beau moved to help, and I waved him away. "I'm fine, really. By tomorrow I'll be good as new."

"Paige, wait," Flora said quietly.

I slid to the floor and wrapped a towel around my waist, limping toward the door. She called my name again, more urgently this time, but I ignored it.

And by the time I made it to my room, fingers trembling and throat aching, I could almost convince myself that leaving them was for the best.

7

THROUGH THE WALL

I STARTLED AWAKE FROM A TROUBLED SLEEP, HEART RACING IN my chest.

I cocked my head to listen but didn't hear a thing. Even the snowy landscape outside had stilled, the storm's aftermath leaving a clear, starry sky in its wake. After I'd clumsily fled the hot tub, I'd taken a quick shower then hopped into bed. When I finally fell into a fitful sleep, Beau and Flora had lingered in my dreams, their hands on my body, their lips on my skin.

A sound drifted in from the hallway. Hushed voices, almost angry sounding.

No, not the hallway.

Beau and Flora's bedroom.

I slipped out of bed and limped as quietly as I could to my door, pushing it open and wincing as it creaked. Silence had fallen again, and as I peered out into the darkened hallway, all I could see was the faintest shimmer of lights from the Christmas tree. The fire had long since been put out, our dishes drying in the sink, the hot tub covered.

There it was again—frantic whispers and someone

saying *shhh*. Goosebumps shivered down my arms as I neared their closed door, my ears straining. I could make out their voices now—Beau's husky drawl, Flora's throaty murmur. Another clash of whispers.

Then I heard my name. Once, then twice. My spine stiffened. Everything after that was too muffled to really understand, but the tone was obvious.

They were arguing.

My fingers flew to my mouth, stomach coiled into knots. I made my way back to my room as quickly as I could, shutting the door tight behind me. I perched on the edge of my bed with a heavy sigh, mentally calculating every mistake I'd made since we arrived. Thought about the gnawing suspicion I'd had that their relationship was in trouble, a suspicion that grew by the hour. Thought about their individual confessions to me, how eager they seemed to remind me that we'd shared a connection once.

Flora asking me about regret. Beau admitting his jealousy.

Was this what Dorothy had done? Bided her time as my relationship with Em began to deteriorate, waiting for the right moment to intervene?

Except I wasn't trying to split them up. I was trying to keep them both. And I couldn't figure out what they were doing.

Behind me, through the wall, came a creaking sound— mattress springs and bodies adjusting. I sucked in a breath and went completely still. My eyes tracked up to the ceiling, and in the dim moonlight, I could make out a grate connecting my room with theirs.

The mattress creaked again, and I heard it, crystal clear, through the grating. A flush crept up my neck at the intimacy of it all, their bodies shifting a few inches from where I sat. Then came hoarse murmurings—affectionate-sounding, not the harsh consonants of their argument. I heard Beau's voice, but still couldn't make out the words.

Next—a moan, low and desperate-sounding.

I froze. My heart rattled my ribcage. From the grate came heavy, labored breathing. More whispers. Another moan, louder this time. After an entire day spent watching them barely touch each other, let alone make direct eye contact, and now...*and now*...

Twisting onto my knees, I shuffled to the top of the bed and pressed my ear directly to the wall before I could talk myself out of it. The world shrank around me. Beau's voice filtered through. "You're gonna come on my tongue, darlin'. But only if you stay quiet. Do you understand?"

I collapsed in total shock.

Flora let out a breathy *please*. Was she naked in their bed, golden limbs striped with hazy moonlight? Was Beau pinning her legs down, opening her wide for his mouth? In my mind, I could see Beau's back and shoulders rippling with ink and muscles as he knelt before her, all crooked grin and arrogance. And I knew the exact second that his tongue touched her clit because she gasped out his name.

I slipped my hand between my legs and pressed on my clit. Another action driven purely by lust, more instinct than rational decision. Flora's next sounds were stifled but increasing in frequency. They were gorgeous, tempting, sinful.

"Yes, that's it." She sighed. "Harder...harder."

Sensation coursed through me. My body was already clamoring for release, driving me to the edge. My nipples were tight against the cool wall, and every drag had my fingers moving faster. I couldn't stop picturing Flora's spine arching off the bed, hands in Beau's hair, her hips rocking in circles as he licked her.

She gave a loud, satisfied moan—quickly muffled. I imagined Beau's large palm pressing to her mouth, keeping her quiet. Envisioned her bucking against his tongue as she orgasmed. Just the *suggestion* of her climax had my own rushing through me so forcefully that I toppled backward onto the bed. At the last second, I shoved a pillow over my face and cried out into it. Getting off on hearing Flora.

Getting off on the idea that they might have heard me too.

But I'd hardly caught my breath before I heard a rhythmic rocking sound. I was back at the wall in an instant. Beau's rough grunt had me sliding my fingers deep inside myself, pretending it was his cock stretching me.

Flora whispered, "Oh my god," and the rhythm picked up.

"If you won't stay quiet, I'll flip you over and press your pretty face into this mattress," he growled.

"You know I won't," she taunted. Then came a chorus of movements and creaks, and my mind filled with the filthiest of images. Flora, naked and on her hands and knees. Beau behind her, hips thrusting against her thighs, his throat exposed as his head tipped back.

I could hear the unmistakable sound of flesh on flesh. It was Beau, fucking Flora from behind on the other side of this wall.

My fingers moved faster. Every time my palm nudged my clit, I had to bite back my own moans.

"So close, so close," Flora begged, completely out of breath. "*Please.*"

He sped up. Their bed knocked against the wall that separated us. I ground against my palm and started to completely unravel. Flora released a muted cry, and Beau's satisfied groan had me coming in rapid spasms.

This time, I fell back onto the bed and stayed there, too wrung out to do much more than chase my own breath. Cloaked in wintry darkness, with only the soaring mountains as witnesses, there was an illicit pleasure in submitting to my forbidden desires. Of feeling *good* and not just conflicted.

Still, when I heard their bedroom door open a few minutes later, I went rigid beneath the sheets. Waited as two sets of footsteps walked to the bathroom, then two sets returned, stopping outside of my room. They hovered, and I waited, and every fiber of my being yelled at me to *say something*.

But after a few taut seconds, they left.

And I was alone in my bed again.

8

DID YOU HEAR US LAST NIGHT?

THE NEXT MORNING, I SLIPPED DOWN THE HALLWAY, ALREADY filled with the scents of cinnamon and butter and roasting coffee. Beau and Flora's bedroom door was partially open, and I paused there. Everything I'd done last night sent a sticky flash of embarrassment through my body, especially since I'd woken up satisfied, practically *relaxed*. The sliver of open door revealed a passed-out, clearly naked Beau with one arm thrown behind his head and the sheets rumpled around his hips. I could see the tattoos on his ribcage, the rise and fall of his bare chest, his disheveled hair.

You're gonna come on my tongue, darlin'. But only if you stay quiet. Do you understand?

I kept walking, needing to shake off the white-hot fever dream of Beau and Flora having sex in the room directly next to mine. In the kitchen, I poured myself a steaming mug of coffee and peered out into a landscape made anew. The world outside was hushed and quiet, suspended in place on the very last day of the year. Idyllic piles of snow shone beneath a brilliant azure sky, surrounded by now-visible mountains. The sunlight sparkled in the nearby pine trees, and in the distance, I could hear the swift trill of bird song.

I cut and ate a slice of gingerbread cake, then wandered into the main room, coming up short when I realized Flora was curled up on the couch by the Christmas tree. She gave me no effervescent greeting or beaming grin. Instead, she was peering at the fire with a furrow in her brow, face drawn as she chewed on the tip of her thumb. Her hair was loose and slightly tangled, and the collar of her sweatshirt hung off her shoulder, revealing the fine lines of her collarbone.

My stomach dropped, remembering what sounded like an argument last night.

"Flor?" I said, head cocked.

She stirred, blinking, and offered up a tiny smile. "Mornin', babe. How's that ankle?"

I flexed it in front of me, noting only the slightest twinge. "Good as new or close to it. Also, happy New Year's Eve, hey?"

That got her smile to widen. "Why, thank you. It's only the *best day of the whole year*."

"So I've heard. Got any new and enchanting possibilities you want to explore?"

One brow winged up. "Maybe. But I can't ruin the surprise. You'll have to wait and find out."

Then she patted the spot next to her, and I obeyed, a little surprised when she nuzzled into my chest for a hug. My arms came around her—the coffee staying in my mug but just barely—and I dropped my nose to the crown of her head. She smelled slightly of Beau, slightly of sex, like musk and sweat. It set off a craving so strong my arms tightened around her reflexively.

"Hey, you okay?" I asked. "Did something happen?"

"Bit of a rough night, but I'm better now," she murmured, pulling away but keeping our legs entwined.

I brushed the hair from her eyes. "I heard...well, this is kind of embarrassing, but I woke up last night and thought I heard you and Beau...arguing?"

A blush darkened her cheeks. "Oh, uh...no. We weren't arguing, but I'm sorry if we woke you up. It was more of an intense conversation is all."

"Do you want to talk about it?" I asked lightly. Internally, I was a twisted knot of conflicting wants and needs. *Please tell me what's going on. Don't tell me what's going on. Please don't break up. Please want me for real.*

Her gaze slid back to the fire. "I've been thinking about what we talked about yesterday. About whether your clients regretted getting married. I know you said you were sure some of them did, but did *you* ever secretly feel like they were making a mistake?"

Those knots in my belly twisted tighter and tighter. "Are you asking if I feel that way about you and Beau?"

She shrugged, looking a little sheepish. "I'm just curious."

I set my coffee down and worked to keep my voice sounding pleasant and not devastated. "You and Beau are meant for each other. Anyone who's around you for more than a minute can see that. And you're not getting married for the status symbol or to feel superior. You're taking up space, declaring your big queer love for the world to see and doing it in front of the people you love the most."

I expected to see her relieved. But she only tipped her head to one side, staring at me like I was the missing puzzle piece she'd been searching for. "We all deserve a celebration like that. A gigantic, splashy party filled with glitter and dancing and reckless abandon. *You* deserve to declare your big queer love to the world too."

"I know I do," I said quickly. "I'd love to start planning more than weddings and commitment ceremonies. I want to help with adoption ceremonies and coming out parties, celebrating anything people want. It shouldn't have to be only milestones. Sometimes the most ordinary of days are the sweetest. What if we danced with reckless abandon on a warm Tuesday in October just because the leaves are changing and it's beautiful?"

"*What if*, indeed," she said. "Is that the kind of wedding that you want? Something fun and freeing on an ordinary day in October?"

I hesitated, weighing which truths I could admit here. Unlike many of my clients, I'd only ever fantasized about the *person* I'd be marrying that day.

Or people.

"I'm not sure I can have the wedding that I want," I said as a blush crept up my throat. "Planning weddings for other people brings me a lot of joy though."

Flora studied me for a long moment. Then she propped one elbow on the back of the couch and dropped her fingers to my open palm, sliding them to my inner wrist. She began stroking tender circles there, setting my nerve endings aflame.

"Is it because of what you said yesterday? That you feel skittish?" she asked.

My eyes were glued to the circular movement of her fingers on my skin. "I'm not..." I swallowed. "I'm not sure what I want is possible."

Silence settled between us, broken only by the crackling of the fire. Those circles had a mesmerizing quality on my entire being, the movements so sensual I had to press my thighs together.

"Paige," she said softly, "were you awake after you heard us talking last night?"

"Yes," I whispered.

Her other hand landed beneath my chin, lifting my eyes to tether onto hers. "Did you hear us?"

If you won't stay quiet, I'll flip you over and press your pretty face into this mattress.

I managed a short nod. This close, Flora's beauty was captivating on a level I failed to understand.

Those fingers on my wrist traced up my inner forearm, up to curve around the ball of my shoulder, the side of my throat. Then she cupped my cheek, thumb dragging along my lower lip. "I wanted you to hear us," she said. "Wanted you to touch yourself on the other side of that wall."

The thrum between my legs became a raging drumbeat.

"And I know you did," she continued, "because we heard you."

A creeping flush engulfed my face. I'd been foolish to assume I could restrain myself, could somehow stifle the pleasure that ripped through me like a cyclone, demolishing every last barrier I'd carefully constructed. My unwieldy feelings for Beau and Flora resisted my every attempt at control, so it only made sense that my desire, too, was a wild and rebellious thing, refusing to do my bidding.

"What...what did you hear?" I asked.

Flora brushed her nose against mine. "We heard you come. Twice, if I'm not mistaken. And I wish you could have *seen* Beau when he did. God, just the *sounds* turned him into some kind of animal. Like a man possessed."

My eyes rose to Flora's, and the sweet inevitability of this moment had me grasping at a thread of courage. "Do you think about me when you fuck him? Do you...do you *both* think about me?"

Understanding dawned on her face. "Oh, sweetheart, you have no idea."

Then she captured my mouth in a kiss, sinking against me as her hands fisted in my curls. Her lips were hot, unyielding, the low hum from the back of her throat sending goosebumps along my skin. My heart galloped at the pure shock of it, causing me to gasp and break our mouths apart.

We panted, our eyes locked together. Flora's coy flirting had vanished, leaving worry and tenderness in its place. My galloping heart spun at this glimpse of vulnerability, the fear that she'd ruined something precious. I knew that fear as intimately as my own breath, had been battling it for two years now.

So I kissed her back. And this time, we didn't break apart. She moaned again as I deepened the kiss, my hands coming up to hold her face. I took her lush mouth, licking my tongue against hers. With a twist of my hair, she tipped my head to the side, dragging her lips down my throat.

"You taste so *fucking* good. I always knew you would," she breathed, then fused our mouths back together. I whimpered, swept away on a wave of ravenous lust. Flora shoved me back against the cushions and climbed onto my lap, straddling me. Our lips didn't stop moving, each kiss filled with so much liberated longing that my head started to spin.

My hands moved beneath her sweatshirt. Her skin was soft as my fingers roamed up to her ribcage. She shivered against me, nipping at my bottom lip as I cupped her breasts. Her head fell back, and I kissed a hot path down her neck, gritting my teeth at the euphoria of her nipples tight against my palms. She ground her hips down against mine, kissing me with a new ferocity.

Flora kept making these needy sighs that had me willing to give her every-fucking-thing in this *world* that she wanted —my mind, my body, my eager heart. Every sun-kissed daydream and lurid fantasy.

A creak of floorboards came from our left, and we jumped in surprise. It was Beau, standing at the foot of the couch in just his sweatpants, wearing that mysterious expression I'd seen so many times before. Lust, yearning, an almost feral possessiveness. Every single atom in my body screeched to a halt—my lungs, my hands, my stupid goddamn brain.

"Beau, you're...hello, uh...good morning," I stammered. Guilt surged through me like a knife, this resounding, dreadful acceptance of how far we'd fucked up. The *one* thing I'd said I'd never do—be like Em and Dorothy—and here I was, breaking all the rules.

Beau raked a hand through his hair, a devilish grin sliding up his face. "Good morning to you too, Paige," he drawled. "Now what are you doing kissing my fiancée?"

9

GIVE PAIGE WHAT SHE DESERVES

Beau closed the distance between us, sliding onto the couch. Flora still straddled my lap, and my fingers flexed beneath her sweatshirt, holding her by the waist. I sat, dazed, as he reached for her face and dragged her forward, crashing his mouth against hers. I had a front-row seat to this kiss, was so close I could watch the muscles working in Beau's jaw. Could see Flora's fingers digging into his hair.

The guilt and shock twisted in my chest, becoming a sharp and hungry craving. I wanted to be Beau kissing Flora. To be Flora, kissing Beau. Wanted to be between them, with them, part of all of it. Every press of their mouths held the shape of a demand, a plea, a cry for release. His chest rumbled on a gravelly moan, and Flora gasped, sighing as he wrapped his hand around her throat. It seemed they shared a single, ragged breath, then Beau pressed his forehead to Flora's.

"I love you, darlin'," he said. "More than I could ever say in this lifetime."

Her smile was sweet, infused with light. "I love you too, so very much."

My heart lodged itself between my ribs. And when Beau turned to face me, my disbelief must have been obvious. He brushed a wayward curl from my eyes, and his fingers trembled against my skin.

"You're not...you're not mad at me?" I asked.

"I could never be mad at you," he said, throat bobbing as he swallowed. "Though I am nervous."

Like with Flora, this glimpse of vulnerability had hordes of butterflies floating through my entire body.

"But I could have sworn you were..." I glanced between the two of them, awestruck. "You're not *breaking up*?"

Beau ducked close and held my gaze. "No, we're not breaking up. And I know we've been acting strange, which we're truly sorry for. We didn't know how to tell you, and our fear got in the way."

"Tell me what?" I said, barely a whisper.

He gripped my face, holding me like I was the most precious thing in his life. "That you've been our undoing, our obsession, our every dream and fantasy. We're in love with you, Paige, and always have been."

My very world tipped and shattered, sending my thoughts flying in a million directions. "This, right here, is everything I ever wanted. But I never thought it was possible."

Flora squeezed my hand. "We could make it possible. The three of us. Together."

I was nodding before she finished speaking, tears tracking down my cheeks. "Yes, *please*. I love you both so much—"

Beau kissed me then. It was hard and almost *angry*, the kind of kiss that sucks the breath from your lungs and turns your body liquid. His fingers tightened against my face before sliding back to grasp my hair, tilting my head and opening me wider, deeper, with those sinfully full lips. My nails bit into his bare shoulders, and he shuddered.

There was a second mouth on me—Flora, her mouth traveling down my neck as Beau continued to ravish me. A lightning bolt of pure ecstasy shot through my body. His hands in my hair, her hands palming my breasts. It was already too much and not enough, painful in equal measure.

Flora swiped her thumbs across my nipples. I moaned, breaking apart from Beau, and she tipped my face toward her and kissed me instead. She teased me with her tongue as Beau's harsh breath coasted along my collarbone. Then his mouth, closing around my nipple and sucking it through the fabric. My hips shot an inch off the couch. Beau released a tortured-sounding growl and his hands tangled in my shirt, pushing upward.

"Everything off, now," he commanded. "We need to see you beneath all these fucking layers."

My sweatshirt went flying, leaving my chest bare to their hungry eyes.

"You've seen me naked before. Or close to it," I pointed out in a daze.

"Not like this," Flora said. "Not when you're *ours*."

She began working my sweatpants down my legs, tearing them off. I was entirely exposed in front of them and vibrating all over from the sheer force of my lust and how desperately my heart surged at their words.

Not like this. Not when you're ours.

You've been our undoing, our obsession, our every dream and fantasy.

We're in love with you, Paige, and always have been.

It was beyond my wildest imaginings, to be wanted and desired and *loved* by them both. My brain couldn't keep up, not with Beau's fingers trailing up my left thigh and Flora's up my right. Two knuckles gave a teasing stroke along my pussy—the *barest* brush, more suggestion than actual action. I hissed in a breath, already clenching. And after exchanging a look, they ducked their heads. Then they were on my breasts, together, and I was officially *gone*.

Beau sucked my nipple between his lips, swirling the tip with his tongue. Flora lapped at my right with a coy smile. I wound my hand through her hair and held her there while my other splayed across Beau's flexing shoulder blades. So much ecstasy coursed through my body that I couldn't help but squirm, pressing my thighs together, sinking my teeth into my bottom lip.

"Please don't ever stop," I begged.

Beau's mouth found my ear. "We don't plan to. Not now, not ever."

His next kiss was rough, drinking me in. He released me only to pull Flora close and do the same thing. For the first time, I could watch them without fighting an army of complicated feelings. Could appreciate how goddamn sexy they were, allowing my fierce longing to drown out the remaining whispers of jealousy.

When they parted, Beau nipped his teeth at her jaw. "I need you naked, Flor. I want our girl to see how beautiful you are."

And beautiful she was. Flora disrobed with all the grace of a ballet dancer, stunning me into silence. Her honey-blond hair fell around her shoulders, drawing my eyes to her small breasts, her delicate tattoos, the flare of her hips and the freckles on her chest. With a sly smile, she hinged forward and kissed me, our tongues sliding together.

Beau's mouth was pressed to the nape of my neck, his pleased groan vibrating against my skin. Reluctantly dragging myself from her mouth, I took Flora's nipple between my lips. Increased the suction while moving my tongue in tight circles. Eyes closed, blissed out, I was aware of nothing but Flora's taste, her smell, her soft skin.

Her fingers curled in my hair, and the cry she let out almost made me come on the spot. Behind me, Beau was gliding up my throat, nipping at my jaw, palming my breasts. I was trapped between them. Giving pleasure. Receiving pleasure. It was an endless loop of desire I never wanted to end.

I propped my chin on her chest, staring up at her as I slipped my fingers between her thighs. She was so wet already, so fucking *hot*.

"I need to make you come," I rasped. "Please, Flora. Let me."

Beau closed his teeth around my earlobe and tugged. I shivered all over, turning to catch his mischievous grin. "Not yet, you don't. Flor's been patiently waiting to eat your pussy for two years now."

The woman in question stepped out of my arms and pushed me back against Beau's chest, wearing a similarly impish grin. He pressed his face into the crook of my neck and curled his big, tattooed hands around my thighs, pinning me down and holding me open as Flora fell to her knees.

"Beau's right," she said, staring at my cunt. "And now that I'm finally seeing you, you're lovelier than I ever thought possible."

My chest was already heaving, my vision gone blurry. Then her mouth descended, blowing light breaths against my feverish skin. My hips canted forward, seeking her touch. Beau soothed me by cupping my breasts, and my head fell back with a sigh. The warmth of her breath was near my clit—close, then a little closer still. He caught Flora's chin between his fingers, tugging down her lower lip.

"You know what to do," he said, his voice low and dangerous. "Be a good girl and give Paige what she deserves."

"Yes, *sir*," she said with a grin. Flora hovered over my slick skin then gave me a long, indulgent swipe. I wasn't sure who groaned the loudest, all three of us riveted on the tip of her pink tongue fluttering on my clit.

"Oh my god," I sighed, head lolling back against Beau's chest. He grabbed my arms and looped them around his neck while Flora pushed my knees even wider apart, leaving me completely exposed and at their mercy. His hands curved up my ribs to palm my breasts. Flora made tiny circles around my clit that had my back arching.

His lips found my ear again as he pinched my nipples. I wanted to squirm, wanted to writhe beneath the erotic assault, but they held me firmly in place.

"Look how sexy Flora is," he murmured, "on her knees for you, that gorgeous face between your thighs. Is this how you like to be licked?"

Flora flattened her tongue and rolled it, sending a galaxy of stars bursting across my vision. I cried out her name, and she smiled.

"Yes, *yes*," I whined. "Just like that, she's...she's perfect."

A sound of approval rumbled in his chest. "She once told me she touches herself and thinks of you like this— held open for her mouth, pinned down to play with. Isn't that true, darlin'?"

"Very true," Flora said, "except she tastes better than all my fantasies."

She swiped her fingers through my pussy then held them up for Beau. He leaned forward, took the digits between his lips and hollowed out his cheeks. His guttural growl had the hair on my arms standing straight up.

He gripped the back of my neck with a pained look in his eyes. "I can't believe we waited this long to taste you. Never again, Paige, you understand? Say the fucking *word* and you'll bring us both to our knees."

He kissed me with a fury, drinking in every moan as Flora swirled her tongue at my opening.

"Can I fuck you now?" she murmured.

"Yes, now, *please*," I begged. Flora pressed one, then two fingers, inside me and started to move, fucking me with short, fast strokes. She licked me harder, and I thrashed against Beau, babbling incoherently as they took me higher and higher. Higher than I'd ever been. My approaching orgasm was so intense I feared I wouldn't make it through.

Beau ground his thick, hard cock against my ass.

"*God*, you feel huge," I gasped.

"You have no idea," he hissed. "And I'm gonna spend this entire weekend fucking both of you into the next stratosphere."

He bit the space between my neck and shoulder, claiming me as Flora sent me soaring toward climax.

"Yes...oh fuck...*Flora*," I chanted, starting to break apart beneath her.

"That's right, come for us," Beau praised. "Show us what we missed last night."

And I did—in huge, tsunami-sized waves that had me screaming their names. The pleasure was endless, and I was an absolute mess, trembling with aftershocks. Flora nibbled up my belly, my breasts, my neck.

She gave me a long kiss. "You made my fantasy come

true," she said, stroking my hair. "I wanted that more than anything."

I cupped her face—my beautiful friend, my permanent crush, the woman I dreamed of kissing so many times.

"Stand up," I said, still panting. "Now it's time for *my* fantasies to come true."

10

GOOD GIRL

I STARED UP AT FLORA LIKE SHE WAS SOME ANCIENT GODDESS I was fully prepared to worship—freckles dotting her collarbone, the pretty florals tattooed on her ribs, the scar near her belly button. Grabbing her ass, I dragged her close, until her pussy was inches from my face.

Beau kissed my shoulder. "What do you want, Paige?"

I pressed my face between her thighs and inhaled greedily. "To make Flora come on my tongue."

She widened her stance and arched toward me. I took my first real taste and groaned in satisfaction. She whispered out a *yes*. So I squeezed her ass roughly and gave her clit a very deliberate swipe.

Beau fisted his hand in my hair and yanked me back. The sharp tug sent a jolt of awareness through me. "Not so fast. I need to tell you what Flora likes, don't I?"

I nodded, my eyes glued to Flora's, my body caged in by Beau's thick thighs. Fingers still in my hair, he guided my mouth forward, back to where I longed to be. "She likes when you start out slow. Make her wait a little."

Flora huffed out a raspy laugh. "He's lying, Paige. Don't

make me wait." But as soon as I began taking lazy, deliberate licks around her clit, she shuddered and sighed. "Actually, never...never mind. What you're doing. Keep...*fuck*, keep doing that."

Beau nuzzled my neck. "I once kept this beauty on edge for an hour, remember that, Flor?"

"Oh god," she panted. She pressed into me, and I moaned, relishing her salty scent. "I remember being so....so *pissed* at you."

"You also came four times that night, so what's there to be mad about?" Beau said, the arrogant grin obvious in his voice.

I kept licking and licking, drunk on Flora's feel, drunk on the power of pleasuring her like this.

Beau tipped forward and his cock pressed more firmly against my ass. I ground back, as much as I was able, and he sucked in a breath.

"Can Paige use her fingers on you?" he asked.

Flora bit her lip and nodded. I thrust two fingers inside her pussy, and she started clenching immediately. My head swam as arousal rushed through me. I needed to come again just minutes after my last climax shattered me from the inside out.

"Now this is what she really likes," he murmured at my ear. "Keep fucking her and licking that clit for me." Then he reached around and slid his fingers behind her body. I couldn't see where they ended up, but based on her gasp of happiness I could guess.

"Flor loves this. Teasing her ass, just enough to make her go wild. Filling her, licking her, worshiping her." Beau kissed the side of my neck. "We can give this to her any time she asks for it."

The faster I moved my tongue, the more I squirmed

between Beau's thighs. I was starting to think I was going to come, hands-free. Flora pushed into my face, greedy for everything I could give her.

"*God*, I'm so close," she sobbed. "I'm so...I'm so...*oh my god.*"

Flora screamed, and Beau and I barely managed to keep her standing. Her inner muscles clenched around my fingers as her lower body shook and her head fell forward. When she eventually collapsed to her knees, she dropped her head onto my legs, panting and laughing.

I brushed the sweaty hair from her cheeks, and when she smiled up at me, my heart just about burst from my chest. I'd spent all this time feeling never truly satisfied, never truly at ease, always desiring the two people that I couldn't have.

Now I had them and it was real.

Please let it be real.

Beau stroked Flora under the chin. She ducked and bit his thumb with a playful look in her eyes.

"You okay, darlin'?" he said with a laugh.

"More than okay. I'm *euphoric*," she replied. "And we want to make you feel that way too."

"Is that right?"

Her gaze darted to mine, as if seeking my approval. The gesture, and the weight of her casual *we*, had that same blush creeping up my neck.

I brushed my lips across Beau's cheek. "What would make you euphoric, Beau?"

Those green eyes darkened. "You, Paige."

The next thing I knew, Beau was gently untangling himself from our bodies and pushing to stand. He was thick and hard beneath his sweatpants, and I hungrily tracked the way the fabric stretched to accommodate him. Flora stood too, squealing as Beau hauled her up around the waist with one arm. He presented me with his other hand and a wolfish grin.

I let him tug me down the hallway on legs that quivered. Once inside, he tossed Flora onto the bed and prowled up the length of her body. Her knees were splayed open, her head thrown back as he pressed kisses up her belly and between her breasts. When he reached her mouth, he took it roughly, eagerly, her nails biting into his shoulders. I couldn't stop staring at his hips, the way he ground against her in these seductive, sinuous movements.

I must have been frozen in place by sheer horniness alone for longer than I realized. Beau turned his head toward me. Arched a single imperious eyebrow.

"Come here. Now," he demanded. "And I want those legs wide for me."

Beckoned by his haughty tone, I crawled across the bed while they assessed me like I was the meal they intended to devour together. When I reached them, Beau dropped to his knees on the floor, grabbed me by the waist and yanked me to the edge. Flora pinned me down by the shoulders and my stomach clenched with anticipation. I was already wet and shuddering beneath his feral appraisal—top lip curled, his throat working, his muscles rippling with tension.

"What...what are you going to do to me?" I asked.

He shoved a lock of hair from his forehead and used his palms to press my thighs even wider. "I'm gonna fuck you with my tongue until you can't remember your own name. Use my mouth to make you realize how much we've wanted you. For how long we've *needed* you."

The agonized groan that followed those words set my body on fire. His fingers dug into my skin, like he was barely hanging on to whatever control he had left. "Seeing you, but not touching you. Being close to you, but never having you. Feeling so frustrated, Flor and I were losing our goddamn *minds.*"

I sought Flora at this admission. Her response was to take my nipple into her mouth, eyes shut in quiet ecstasy, pulling firmly as my spine arched off the bed. "You're our wildest dreams come true, Paige," she whispered around my skin. I whimpered, overwhelmed by it all. "Everything we ever hoped for and more."

With a hushed growl, Beau's hot mouth was finally on me. His tongue darted out and circled my entrance. "Goddammit, you taste so good. I'll never get enough of this."

My body was a forest fire of raging sensation—Beau's rough hands on my skin, his wet tongue, Flora's hot lips on my ear, her soft hair grazing my breasts. Then Beau pushed his tongue all the way inside me, and I cried out his name. He moved in long, generous strokes that had me thrashing against the sheets. Flora captured my mouth and kissed me, moaning as Beau truly devoured me. I clutched at her face and kissed her sloppily. No finesse, no precision, all roaring passion.

My body was one long string being plucked, and every nerve ending sang with delight. Beau's tongue wiggled at a sensitive spot, and my hips shot up. He pinned me back down—smug mischief in his eyes—and used his thumb to circle my clit.

"Oh my god, oh my god, *ohmygod*," I gasped. He did it again, using more pressure this time, and a second mind-blowing orgasm approached at rapid speed. "Beau, I'm gonna...you're gonna make me come."

He tilted my hips, taking even more of me. His tongue lashed inside, his thumb circled, and my vision grew hazy.

Flora angled her body, and I pulled her close, licking her nipples until she shivered in my arms.

"That feels so good, Paige," she panted. "I want your mouth on me when Beau gets you off."

And get me off he did.

His tongue slipped from my channel and curled at my clit. That was all it took. I wailed between Flora's breasts as I climaxed for what felt like forever. When I finally came back down, I blinked my bleary eyes open to the sight of Beau standing up.

And slipping off his sweatpants.

A bead of sweat slid down his stomach, and his muscular thighs rippled with tattoos. His cock was thick and heavy as he fisted it, squeezing tight. And then he was crawling up my body with a predatory gleam in his eyes and a determined set to his sinful mouth. He used his arms to cage me in and rock his cock against my still-sensitive clit.

I gasped, and he stole a kiss, breathing me in and pushing the tangled hair from my face. The kiss grew harsher. Hungrier. Beau tasted like me, and I tasted like Flora, and the combination was its own kind of euphoria.

"I forgot my own name, just like you said," I sighed.

"You're such a good girl for me," he ground out. "And you are so fucking beautiful it hurts."

I glowed beneath his praise. Wanted to preen at the way he studied my face with obvious devotion. But then Beau turned and kissed Flora, lengthening the moment until they were smiling. My throat tightened at the sight of their easy affection, my body crying out for that kind of intimacy even after being so thoroughly fucked and pleasured by them both.

Until their lips landed on either side of my face, Flora kissing down my neck while Beau trailed kisses through my hair. He kissed me, then she did, battling to press their mouths to mine. When they finally stopped, I was a wilting mess of the softest feelings.

How loved they made me feel already—to hear them tell it, I'd consumed their every waking thought as they'd consumed mine.

No wonder this felt so natural, so good, so *very right*.

Flora nudged her nose against Beau's. "I want to watch you fuck Paige now."

His body tensed at her words, though his hips kept grinding down in those hypnotic circles. I smoothed my hands over his round, muscular ass. Sank my nails into the skin as he hissed through his teeth.

"Don't go easy on me, Beau. I can take it."

His eyes searched mine, the intensity blazing. One tattooed hand landed on my throat, fingers encircling with a careful strength. "I've thought about this moment so many times I went fucking *mad* over it. So yeah, you're gonna take everything I give you, Paige."

I bit my nails into his ass again, and his nostrils flared. "*Please* fuck me. I need it."

"Condom or no condom? Flora and I have only been with each other, but we were also tested recently."

"Me too," I said, nodding eagerly. "And I'm on the IUD. So please, for the love of god—"

Beau thrust forward, stretching me inch by inch with what seemed to be the last of his willpower. His muscles twitched with restraint, and his neck shimmered with sweat. So much ecstasy was coursing through my body that when he finally bottomed out, I was already sky-high. Nothing but a cloud of delirious elation and slick desire.

Beau's forehead dropped to mine, and he exhaled roughly through his nose. "Paige...*Christ*, you feel fucking incredible." He pulled almost all the way out, then rocked back inside. Gently at first, a full-on tease, then increasing the rhythm of his strokes. "I love feeling you clench around me. Love knowing that Flora fucked you first, that she got to feel you like this too. So tight, so *wet* for us, aren't you?"

A whimper fell from my lips. "Yes...always. I always am."

His body slapped against mine—harder and harder and harder—and I wasn't sure I'd survive this next onslaught. When he hooked my knee higher, his cock rubbed every sensitive spot. "Did you enjoy the little show Flor and I put on for you last night?"

My spine arched, and he dipped his head, tonguing my nipples. "Yes...*god*...yes, I did. I...I loved it."

When he kissed me, he used his teeth to tug down my lip, marking me. "Did hearing Flora come with my mouth between her legs get you off?"

I nodded, half sobbing, my chest heaving. Beau planted his hands on either side of my face, and his hips swiveled, his cock so deep I really was forgetting my name, forgetting *everything*. All my fears, my many anxieties and concerns. I was nothing but a body bound between Beau and Flora, each of us driving toward release.

He hovered his mouth at my ear, running his tongue along the shell. "Do you know how hard it was for us to hear you through that wall and not come crawling to you on our hands and knees? How hard it was to wait *again* to make you ours?"

I was trembling with the need to come. "I wanted..." I panted, "I wanted you to take me, to use me, to make your fantasies come true."

"*This* is what we wanted," he growled. "You, with us. Between us. All of us together, for hours, for days, for years."

My mouth opened wide as my head lolled from side to

side. Flora stretched out next to me, her naked body lithe and beautiful. She pressed a curved purple sex toy against her pussy and turned it on. Her teeth sank into her bottom lip, but her eyes stayed fixed on our moving, grinding bodies. Beau balanced his weight on one arm so he could palm her breast, rolling her nipple between his fingers.

She sucked in a breath. "Watching you two together is so fucking hot. Tell me how good his cock feels, Paige."

"I'm so full," I gasped. "He's so...he's so *big*."

Beau surged between my legs and ground his pelvis against my clit. I seized up, poised to break apart.

"I need to feel you coming on my cock, gorgeous," he murmured against my lips. "Give it to me."

I hurtled off the edge and absolutely exploded. My vision went dark, and every single thought vanished. Next to me, Flora moaned through her own orgasm, and Beau fucked me in quick, rough strokes. When he came—mouth on mine, one hand gripping my throat—his rumbling, satisfied groan had me shivering.

Beau shoved the hair from my face and dragged his nose along my temple, breathing me in. He shifted to the side, making room for Flora to curl up on my chest while he draped a heavy arm over us both, pulling us tight. Sweat coated our limbs, and our breathing stayed unsteady.

I felt absolutely wrung out and overwhelmed with all that we'd done.

Of all that we'd said.

We couldn't take it back, couldn't pretend that it didn't matter. Too many vulnerable truths had been spilled. Too many secrets had come to light.

All of us together.
For hours. For days.
For years.

11

NEW AND ENCHANTING POSSIBILITIES

I DRIFTED AWAKE STILL PRESSED BETWEEN BEAU AND FLORA. The winter sun had risen higher in the sky, but I was cocooned and cozy in their body heat. Flora was wrapped around my front and Beau curled around me from behind. His breath feathered the nape of my neck, his chest hair was coarse against my skin, and his cock, semi-hard even in sleep, was a distracting presence.

I let my lips dance along the top of Flora's head. Ran my fingers through her tangled hair. Skimmed my palm between her shoulder blades then followed the dip of her waist, the curve of her thigh hitched around mine. Before, every touch between the three of us felt like a false promise. A stolen moment to feel guilty about instead of enjoy. But our secrets had been dragged into the sunlight, laid bare and handled with exquisite care.

It was as thrilling as it was terrifying.

Flora stirred awake beneath my touch. She gave a feline stretch then blinked her eyes open, wearing a sleepy smile that had me leaning in to kiss her. Because I wanted to.

Because I could.

I'd meant for the gesture to be sweet, but Flora arched against me and deepened the kiss. Our mouths moved slowly, sensually. Learning each other, tasting each other, enjoying the delicious feel of our naked limbs entwined. I fisted my hand in her hair and tugged, angling her face up so I could kiss along her throat. She shivered and rocked into me, pressing her pussy against my thigh.

And suddenly I had a second set of hands roaming my body. Beau's gravelly chuckle vibrated against my hair.

"She wasn't a dream, Flor," he rumbled. "She's real."

His fingers found my chin, turning me so I could receive another sensual kiss. My back hit the mattress while Flora's tongue teased below my ear.

"Did you...did you think I'd vanish?" I managed.

She hummed. "A little. But you're still here, still ours to play with."

"And how fucking lucky are we to have Paige Presley all to ourselves," Beau drawled. One big hand cupped my breast, pinching my nipple. Flora kissed my belly, moving lower.

I was already squirming beneath their combined focus. "You're not tired?"

Another chuckle from Beau, this one dangerous at the edges. "You don't have to worry about that. We're just gettin' started."

He joined Flora, each holding one of my legs open. They teased along my inner thighs. Kissed my knees, sent their breath coasting across my clit. Every time my hips rolled, they'd push me back down, pinning me. When Flora licked my pussy, I watched Beau's gaze turn starved and ferocious. He nudged her out of the way and did the same thing, until Flora got impatient and stole his spot.

Their tongues were wet and confident, yet different in

their size, the amount of pressure, the speed of their circles. The dual sensations were like nothing I'd ever felt before. If I wanted to, I could have floated my body right to the ceiling, utterly buoyant on sheer pleasure alone.

Flora twisted her fingers in Beau's hair and yanked him back. One eyebrow arched in amusement. "You want me out of the way, darlin'?"

She kissed his cheek with a toothy grin. "You just fucked Paige. I want a turn."

Their eyes slid to mine, and I couldn't help my own teasing smile. I dragged my toes up the ridges of Beau's stomach, the planes of his chest. He grabbed my ankle and pressed an open-mouthed kiss there.

"You heard the lady," I said. "It's her turn. But you can watch."

He closed his teeth around my skin with a playful growl. "I won't survive it."

Flora pushed him back onto the bed with a laugh. He reached for her face, pulling her down for a kiss they smiled around.

"When did you get so bossy?" he asked.

"You love it when I'm bossy," she countered, wrapping her hand around his cock and stroking. He hissed out a breath and groaned. "You can jerk off while you watch. But you can't come until we do."

"Yes, ma'am," he said. And I had only a few seconds to take him in—gloriously naked and reclined on the bed, fingers wrapped around his thick cock and his eyes boring into mine. Then Flora pinned my arms to the bed and straddled my waist. Her blond hair fell in waves around her shoulders, and the strands were soft on my skin when she bent down to kiss me. With our mouths still fused together, she shifted position, aligning her wet cunt onto mine. She gave an experimental thrust, and our clits rubbed together.

"Oh *shit*," I gasped, breaking our kiss.

She bit her lip and smiled. "Is this okay?"

"God, yes." I grabbed her hips and we moved together, another decadent slide of our bodies. Flora reached forward, gripping the headboard. I gazed up at her in sheer wonder, entranced by the sinuous circling of her lower body. Her pink nipples, high and tight. The dreamy expression fixed on her face, every choked moan and whisper. And when I turned my head, Beau's tattooed forearm flexed as his hand worked on his shaft. His breaths were fast, ragged. Arm muscles bunching with the effort.

"She's so fucking gorgeous," he gritted out. "Every time she rides me like that, I lose my damn mind."

Flora's head fell back, exposing the lines of her throat. She kept grinding and grinding against my clit while I was suspended between ecstasy and adoration. She angled her upper body forward so I could touch her breasts, roll her nipples against my palm. The room filled with the sounds of Beau's fist on slick skin and his harsh breathing. The slight creak of the bed, Flora's growing sighs, my own chants as I was reduced to a babbling, obsessed mess. My hold on her hips tightened and I started to thrust up to meet her, each point of pressure coiling tighter and tighter in my belly.

"You feel incredible," she gasped. "I never wanna stop."

She dropped her hands back to the bed and bent over, kissing me until stars exploded through my brain. I rocked her faster on top of my body, my climax hovering at the base of my spine.

"Goddammit, I'm so close," Beau said through clenched teeth. "I've never seen anything as sexy as the two of you together."

Her legs shook as she ground down. "Please come with me," she begged, throwing her head back and grabbing the headboard again. "I need you, Paige."

And that was all it took. A sharp orgasm took me completely by surprise, bowing my spine off the bed as I wailed. Flora followed, chanting "Yes, yes, *yes*," as she trembled through every last tremor. Beau gave his cock one more rough stroke then groaned in relief. His head tipped back, and his come spilled onto his flexing stomach.

Both of them, beautiful.

Both of them...*mine*.

"Oh *fuck*," Flora said with a laugh, collapsing onto my chest as I blinked at the ceiling in dazed wonder.

"Oh fuck is right," he panted. "I'm a ruined man after that."

"Ruined in a good way?" I asked.

He tossed us a crooked grin that lit up the room. "The only way I know how."

My own smile gave way to a freeing laughter, and once I started it was impossible to stop. Flora giggled against my throat. Beau rolled towards us, still grinning, and gave us each a loud, smacking kiss on the cheek.

"Much as I'd hate to leave this bed, I feel it's important as the resident medical professional to make sure we're fed and hydrated," he said, standing and pulling on his sweats. "I shall return with cake, water and pain meds."

"You're my hero, Beau Duvall," Flora said sleepily.

He winked and swaggered out of the room. I gingerly pushed myself to sit against the headboard and snorted when I caught sight of my snarled curls in the mirror. But then my eyes tracked across the bed—our discarded clothing, the bunched sheets, Flora's fingers tangled with mine.

Reality crashed back around me, as jarring as a stack of plates falling off a table.

Beau and Flora weren't breaking up. Beau and Flora *were in love with me.*

I must have made a sound, some gulp of disbelief, because Flora appeared by my side, sweeping the hair from my face.

"Hey," she said, "I know it's a lot. It's a lot for us too. But this wasn't some random fun or a one-time thing for us. We meant every single word that we said. I want you to know that, okay?"

I nodded, releasing a shaky exhale. "Okay. I do and I...I trust you. It all just hit me at once. A dream come true that I assumed was impossible."

Her brown eyes softened. "You were my New Year's Eve wish, by the way. My new and enchanting possibility."

"Oh, Flor," I whispered, breath lodged in my throat.

This next kiss was all sweet affection and poignant memory. It was the kiss that hovered between us beneath my poncho that day, the kiss that threatened to destroy me in that club bathroom. The one I knew would fully unravel us that night on the couch, when Beau lay only a few feet away.

I felt the shiver that wracked her spine when our tongues met. Wanted to worship the whimper she made when my teeth nipped her lower lip. We only parted when Beau returned a moment later, his expression filled with so much reverence I had to duck my head, hiding a blush.

He brushed his lips at my temple, and I felt the shape of his smile.

"Can't leave you two alone for one second, huh?" he teased.

Flora tugged him forward by the waist of his sweatpants.

He smoothed her hair down and kissed the crown of her head. Then he pressed pain meds and glasses of water into our hands. With a flourish, he presented a plate full of gingerbread cake.

"Meds in case you're sore. Water because we're *clearly* dehydrated. And cake for our ravenous hunger."

I gulped down the glass of water and eyed the cream cheese frosting, suddenly fucking *starving*. I moaned around a bite, shaking my head. "Who knew having wild threesome sex with my engaged-to-be-married best friends would work up such an appetite, huh?"

Beau laughed, sliding onto the bed next to us. "Is this how you expected to spend your New Year's weekend?"

I scoffed. "Not in the least. I *expected* to get pretty fucking tipsy at the New Queers Eve dance party and spend most of the night missing you both and wishing you were there."

They paused, mid-motion, to stare at me. My hand flew to my mouth, an absurd attempt to shove the words back inside.

"I'm...sorry," I stammered. "That was weird to say, right?"

But Beau gently grasped my wrist, pulling it free. "It's all different now, Paige. We don't have to pretend around each other anymore. We can tell the truth. And the truth is that if you hadn't gotten trapped here, we would have spent the weekend missing you too."

"Really? Even in this beautiful place, on your special romantic getaway?" I asked.

Flora settled her head in my lap, her long hair spilling everywhere. "Yes, really. You're the missing piece, and you always have been."

So much emotion crowded the back of my throat, I had to focus on my breathing. Beau draped a hand on my knee, stroking my skin with his thumb. "I know Flor and I have been acting real weird the past few weeks and probably been a pain in the ass to boot. We're so sorry about all of it. It was never our intention to make you worry or upset. We were just...confused and scared, is all."

"For the record, I really did think you were breaking up. Or at least in some kind of turmoil," I said. "And that gave me all these...these *complicated* feelings. I never wanted you to break up so I could pursue one of you separately. It was never about that. It was..." I picked at the sheets, unsure of the wording. "It was this, right here. The three of us together, equal and committed."

His hand tightened on my knee. "I like this, right here, a whole hell of a lot."

"Me too," Flora said. "You know, we always had a crush on you, Paige. He and I both, even before we started dating. It was part of who we were as a couple—falling in love with each other while acknowledging we had a totally normal crush on a friend we cared deeply about."

"A big crush," he added. "Gigantic. Enormous. The biggest one the world has ever seen."

I batted my eyelashes to the best of my ability. "An enormous crush on little ol' *me*?"

Flora sat up, and Beau looped an arm around her shoulders, pulling her against his chest as she laughed. "We're infatuated with her, and she barely knows it, Flor," he said. "Looks like we'll have to keep her in this bed until she accepts it."

I let myself get tugged into the other side of his chest, smiling when they tried to kiss me at the same time. "Okay, okay, I believe you. I'm sure it was totally obvious I was obsessed with you too, right?"

"God, we hoped you were," he said. "Because that crush didn't go away. When you moved to California is when we realized how fucking miserable we were without you, missing you more than the way we'd miss a friend. We ached for you, gorgeous. Every day and every night. So much so that when you moved back and started planning our wedding, we finally had to acknowledge what those big, gigantic feelings really were. We were in love with you."

"And we have so many queer friends in all kinds of relationships," Flora added. "We're surrounded by these amazing examples of what romantic love can look like. Poly folks, open relationships, couples who date other couples. Beau and I truly believed our love was expansive. As infinite and vast as the universe. It wasn't about scarcity or deprivation, only this abundant love we never wanted to limit or censor. We'd had plenty of conversations about the topic, but saying '*hey, actually, I also love this other person*' was way more terrifying than all of our philosophical ideas."

"Honestly...I thought I might lose Flora," Beau said hoarsely. "And that scared me shitless. I don't even like thinkin' about it. But hiding what I was feeling felt like the worst kind of betrayal. I just had to figure out how to say, 'I'm in love with Paige but it doesn't make me love you any less. In fact, I love you both *more* because of it.'"

It was like my heart had entered some kind of cartwheel competition. It twirled and spun, rejoicing at hearing my near-constant thoughts reflected back to me.

Not *less,* but *more.* A love that was limitless and all-consuming. I'd been at a loss for words to define how complex my feelings were. It often felt undefinable, even as a person who specialized in planning weddings that celebrated exactly that kind of love. A love beyond boundaries and binaries, a love that rejected all the bullshit societal rules.

Flora pressed her face into Beau's neck. "I don't think

Beau expected me to say, 'wait, you too?' when he confessed he was falling in love with you."

Their shared laughter warmed me like a burst of hot sun on a chilly day.

"I am sorry for not being braver *sooner*. For making you worry and feel confused, Paige," she continued. "The problem with our wedding was never this frivolous quest for a perfect venue. We could care less about any of it. But we didn't want to be in a relationship without *you* in it. And I was terrified that marrying each other would make us lose you. And that telling you the truth might make us lose you too. So instead we were...dragging our heels."

I cocked my head. "And the argument last night?"

Beau scrubbed a hand down his face. "Not an argument necessarily. We'd both spent the day trying to find a way to tell you and completely failed at it. A sudden snowstorm traps us in this cabin together? With no other people and nothing to do but talk? If we didn't tell you here, we never would. But we know what you've been through, especially with Em and Dorothy. We hated the idea of making you feel betrayed or abandoned."

Uneasy tension traveled up my spine. Being loved by Beau and Flora felt too good to be true. Yet I trusted their desire, understood their fears and hesitations because I had plenty of my own. Everything leading up to this moment—here on this bed, surrounded by snowy mountains—was the culmination of a slow, steady burn. The constant heat that had simmered between us from the beginning.

But even though we'd been wrong together in the end... Em had once been too good to be true. So had Dorothy. When I first moved to California, I couldn't imagine my life without them. And they'd still left me.

Quite easily, in fact.

I hated that they still lingered in the back of my thoughts, poking a hole through my hope. But I knew that pretty words meant nothing without actions. If we weren't careful, if we weren't honest, Beau, Flora and I could lose so very much. Our love, our friendship, each other.

And that meant accepting that I deserved their love, this bold and radical thing I helped other people celebrate all the time.

"I love you, Beau," I said. "And I love you, Flora. Have loved you both so much for as long as I can remember."

My breath hitched as Beau dragged me into his lap. He cupped my face and kissed me, that tremble back in his fingers. The kiss was long and thorough, a gesture of relief and joy and gratitude.

When we parted, he murmured, "Say it again."

A smile split my face in two. "I'm in love with you, Beau Duvall."

The look he shared with Flora was so profound, so intimate, that tears threatened to spill over again. I understood that look, when you've finally been given the one thing you ever asked for. He kissed her forehead before letting her sweep me into our own thorough kiss, let her lips smack against my cheek over and over while I laughed.

"You're in *love with me*?" she said.

I brushed her hair back from her face. "Painfully so. But I was as scared as you both. I really did think it was this... this *secret* I could never tell. I assumed you were monogamous, that no matter how much you loved me as a friend it could never be more than that. Thought if I came clean about it and you rejected me, we'd have no reason to stay friends any longer. And that was a future I refused to acknowledge. So it became easier to hide it, easier to pine for you in private, easier to plan your wedding than risk losing you."

Beau smoothed his palm across my back in big, soothing circles. I sagged a little under the weight of all I'd been carrying, a weight they seemed prepared to help me release for good.

"We are monogamous. Or we *were*," Beau said quietly. "Until you. Until we realized we needed to imagine a different kind of life for ourselves. A life with you, if you'll have us."

My mind filled with dozens of questions and scenarios, all my anxieties stacking up like the firewood outside. But I raised my chin and held their gazes, staring at these two people whose courage inspired my own.

"I have a lot of questions. And we have plenty to figure out. But I'm ready to imagine something different, to create something new. Together."

Flora wiped her cheeks and sniffed. "Well then, it's settled. Tonight's New Year's celebration will be extra special. Which means I need to start cooking immediately."

She moved to stand, but Beau caught her hand. "Not so fast, darlin'. I think we deserve a little fun after all that heavy talk."

She arched a dramatic brow. "Yes, sir. And what kind of fun did you have in mind?"

"I'm also interested in that kind of fun," I said.

Beau hugged me to his chest with a rumbling laugh. "Slow down, perverts. We had sex like *seven minutes ago*. I'm talking about something wholesome." He sent his focus to the landscape outside, where soft piles of snow beckoned. "I say we go sledding."

12

THERE'S THE GIRL WE KNOW
AND LOVE

I PUSHED OPEN THE FRONT DOOR AND PEERED OUT ACROSS THE endless expanse of snowy terrain surrounding our cabin. We looked like a trio of astronauts, preparing to space walk on an unforgiving planet. We'd collectively raided the closets for whatever we could find and were now donned in thick snowsuits and sturdy, if ill-fitting, snow boots. There was about an hour of good daylight left, the sky already turning a peachy mauve. The air smelled crisp and evergreen, something like hope filling my lungs.

Flora hefted our makeshift sleds in her arms. They were nothing but trash can lids we'd rescued from the garage, with Beau's express opinion that they created the most aerodynamic speed.

"So I came out here a bit ago and clocked that beauty of a hill right past the cluster of pines," he said, pointing to our left. "It'll be tough getting up but real fucking fun coming down. What do you think?"

"Sounds good to me," I said. "My ankle should be fine to make the trek too."

But he was already shaking his head. "There's no way

I'm letting you trudge up that hill with a busted ankle. Hop on my back and I'll carry ya."

"Neither of you seemed very concerned about my minor injury when you ravished me on the couch earlier."

Flora wrapped her arms around my waist and nipped at my jaw. "I seem to recall you doing a fair amount of ravishing, babe."

"And your ankle was fine," Beau said.

"Were you really paying that much attention? Because my recollection is that you were *very* distracted."

His lazy grin sent a flush to my cheeks. "I was paying close attention to every single inch of your body." Then he dropped to his knees in front of me. "Now hop on my damn back. I'm not askin'."

With a roll of my eyes, I did as I was told, barely able to suppress my complete and utter pleasure at being cared for like this.

He stood, taking me with him, and grabbed my thighs to hitch me higher. "How's that?"

"Would be better if the person carrying me wasn't so insufferable."

He laughed and took Flora by the hand, setting us off toward the hill. "There's the girl we know and love."

I dropped my face to the nape of his neck, breathing him in. Steadying myself against the wave of fluttering feelings those words gave me.

A life with you, if you'll have us.

We began a slow trudge, boots crunching through thick layers of snow. Downed branches and tiny hoofprints littered the path.

"Why did you bring three trash can lids?" I asked. "I assumed we'd all be riding in a sled together."

Beau whistled under his breath. "Shit no, it's a race. The

fastest person down wins and can then claim sled dominance over all the others."

"What on earth is *sled dominance*?" I asked with a laugh.

"It's only Beau's ultimate goal because he's a notoriously sore loser," Flora said.

"How would you know when I've never lost?" he shot back.

She threw a snowball at his chest. He danced away, but it still struck him in the arm, soaking the side of my pants.

"*Gotcha*," she sang.

He wrapped an arm across her chest and yanked her close, kissing the top of her beanie-covered head. "Gotcha back." Then he glanced at me. "And I wanna know why you think sledding was ever something other than a competitive full-contact sport. Who raised you again?"

"Peter and Todd," I said, still laughing. "And you're from *Atlanta*. Do you really think your knowledge of sledding is more than mine? The person born and raised here?"

He hefted me an inch higher. "I've lived here since college. That's ten years of adult-level sledding. I play to win. Every fucking time. And if Peter and Todd are spreading lies, I'll have to correct them at your birthday barbecue."

"Please don't," Flora said. "They're my best customers at the bakery, and I'd love to keep earning an income."

My dads threw me a backyard barbecue every year for my birthday, and they looked forward to seeing Beau and Flora more than anyone else. Had them over for Sunday dinners a few times when I was in California. Visited Flora at the bakery and dropped off food for Beau when he worked long shifts.

Maybe my parents had already sensed the truth of what we were becoming to one another.

Beau set me down gently at the top of the hill, and Flora

handed me a trash can lid. The descent was smooth and steep, the snow barely disturbed.

Flora pointed to a short stump at the bottom. "Last one there is on dish duty tonight."

"Deal," I said.

"Good luck with those dishes," Beau said cheerfully. Then he hopped on his own lid and took off. Flora and I exploded in laughter and outrage. She sailed down immediately after him and I was quick to follow. We careened around sticks and tumbled through drifts of fluffy snow. My body was suffused with a heady buoyancy, a childlike freedom comprised entirely of wet mittens and wind on my face and my surging sled.

Beau flew past the stump well before us—but I lost control at the very end, pitching face-first into them both.

"You...cheated," I said, completely out of breath. "You're a poor loser and a cheater."

"Told ya," Flora said triumphantly.

Beau rose and pulled me up with him. He dusted his gloves across my jacket, shaking off the worst of the wet snow. "All I'm hearing is the sound of two people on dish duty tonight."

I narrowed my eyes. "Best three out of four."

"Are you issuing me a challenge, Paige Presley?"

"Are you scared?"

"He's definitely scared," Flora said in a stage whisper.

He stalked up to us both, giving her, and then me, a swift kiss on the lips. "Too bad I don't get scared."

I snorted. "Sounds like a lot of false bravado to me."

"Oh, I'll prove it," he said. "All spoils to the winner, I say."

"And what are the spoils?" Flora asked.

"You two," he said confidently. Before I could respond,

Beau scooped me against his chest again and began jogging up the way we'd come down. "Come on Flor, I've got three more wins to achieve, and time's a-wastin'."

The next time down, Beau eked out a win, just barely, and celebrated by bending Flora backward in a Hollywood-style kiss. So I used their distraction to my advantage. I scooped up my lid and charged back up the hill as carefully as my ankle would allow.

"Now who's the cheater?" Beau yelled.

"I'm not falling for any of your tricks this time," I yelled back.

A second later, he and Flora were breathless and laughing next to me. All three of us made a sloppy play to make it to the top, half-tumbling, half-lurching back down again in our sleds. We did it again and again. A sixth time, then a seventh, the original bet lost in the joy-filled ruckus as our bodies ricocheted through the air. We were weight-less and ethereal together, as free as I'd felt in years.

And on the eighth trip down, all of us panting and lying together at the finish line, I blurted out, "I moved to California because watching you start to date broke my heart."

They turned to me, their jaunty expressions becoming serious and their hands finding mine.

"I hoped throwing myself into a relationship with someone like Em, someone fun and exciting, would help me get past my feelings for you," I continued. "But all I really did was lock those feelings away, until I saw you again and realized I'd never, not once, stopped loving you. I only said yes when you asked me to plan your wedding because being close to you was always preferable to being apart." I shrugged, wrinkling my nose. "And...apparently I'm a masochist who loves pain."

Beau grabbed the top of my zipper and pulled me

forward, hovering his mouth close. "Then let's make a deal. No more pain. No more lies. No more secrets. Okay?"

I swallowed thickly and nodded. His lips slanted over my own in a kiss that stunned, and I clung to his shoulders as he plundered my mouth. Like he could kiss away every time I'd kept them close while my heart was in anguish.

Flora took my hand and gently tugged off my now-icy gloves. She turned it over, pressing a kiss to my palm, then the inside of my wrist.

"I understand the impulse," she said, caressing my knuckles. "Beau and I at least had each other to love and confide in while you experienced all of this alone. I wish I could take that pain from you, wish I could go back in time and do everything differently. Including not asking you to plan our wedding."

"But I wanted to," I said. "I really mean that."

"You wanted to be around us," she said with a smile. "And when it boiled down to it, that was our motivation as well. We pretended it wasn't for a while, pretended this was just another aspect of our close, intimate friendship with you. Our crush to end all crushes. Then we realized that we couldn't imagine getting married without marrying you too. That's all we want, Paige."

My heart froze like the chilled air around us, a riotous bliss rising in me as her words became clear.

"You want...you want to marry me?" I asked, hardly containing the glee in my voice.

Her eyes filled with tears. "Yes, we very much do."

13

THE SPOILS OF VICTORY

AFTER DRAGGING OUR FREEZING BODIES INSIDE, WE MADE excellent use of the bathroom's giant shower with multiple showerheads. We kissed and teased and tasted each other until our fingers turned to prunes. But through some unspoken agreement, we didn't let each other come, opting instead to stay urgent and grasping and needy.

A new compulsion thrummed between us in the steam.

They want to marry me, they want to marry me, they want to marry me.

After toweling dry in front of the bedroom's crackling fireplace, the three of us stumbled backward onto the bed.

Flora knelt before Beau, winding a red silk tie between her fingers. "Put your arms up and around the headboard."

He arched a cocky brow. "And what exactly did you have in mind?"

"The spoils of your victory." She nipped at his jaw. "Now arms up, Beau. Don't make me tell you again."

"Yes, *ma'am*."

And with a raspy laugh, Beau did as he was told. He was magnificent, splayed out like that—his hands fisted around the metal, his shoulder muscles straining with the effort, his tattooed chest shuddering as Flora tied him up. I dropped to my hands and knees, crawling toward his thick thighs. She kissed down his flexing stomach. I palmed the firm muscles of his legs, sliding my hands up to his cock, jutting out and fully erect.

My mouth watered at the sight.

Her eyes found mine. She tugged my lips to hers, demanding a kiss. I gave and gave, licking into her mouth, squirming as she moaned. Squirming as Beau hissed between his teeth.

"I didn't realize torture was on the menu tonight," he grunted.

"You can pretend you hate it all you want," Flora said with a feline smile. "But Paige and I know what you love."

"Oh yeah? And what's that?"

She ducked her head and took his cock between her pretty cranberry lips. I watched her mouth slide down slowly. Heard her soft moan and Beau's ragged growl. Being endlessly teased by these two in the shower had only amplified the direness of my need for them. This couple that I'd pined for, ached for, loved fiercely.

This couple I was going to marry.

She sped up her movements, taking him deeper and humming as she did so.

"*Fuck*, Flor," he groaned. "You're too good to me."

I reached forward, entranced, and gathered her wet hair in my fist. When I pulled, she moaned again, then released him and said, "Your turn, babe."

My gaze flew up to meet Beau's feral one. His jaw clenched, and the tendons in his forearms were visible as he wrenched at his restraints. I kept our eyes locked together and did the same as Flora, lowering my mouth down as much as I could take. He was thick and salty, stretching my lips. And the sound he made when his cock hit the back of my throat wasn't human. It was raw and desperate, an animal keening that became a chanting of my name.

"Goddamn, you've got a mouth like heaven," he panted.

My toes curled at the worship in his voice, even as he was so clearly on the edge already. I released him and beckoned Flora to join me. We ran our tongues up opposite sides of his shaft, letting our mouths meet in the middle for sloppy kisses.

Beau's hips rose from the mattress, eager for more. I wrapped my fist around the base as Flora took him into her mouth again and hollowed her cheeks. His head tipped back, and beads of sweat dotted his throat. When she lifted her head, I replaced her—tasting Flora on Beau as I took him as deep as I was able. She twisted her fingers in my hair, setting off sharp spikes of pleasure and pain. I moaned and took him deeper, let her hand guide me up and down as Beau writhed on the bed.

When she finally pulled me up, her lips were swollen, eyes heavy-lidded.

"Behind you, in the drawer, is a bottle of lube," she said. "Can you grab it for me?"

I obeyed, handing it over as she shot Beau a smirk. She coated her finger and said, "Do you want to get fucked, Beau?"

"Please, *god*, I'll do anything," he begged hoarsely.

Then he spread his legs wider, giving her greater access. She trailed her finger down his cock and over his balls. Dipped, and then she was pushing her finger inside the tight ring of his ass.

I was utterly captivated and frozen to the spot. Beau

cursed with every thrust of Flora's finger and when she nodded at me, I took him between my lips again.

He strained so hard against the headboard, I worried it might break. The power I had over this man, the power I had over them *both*, sent an electric rush of arousal up my spine. They'd fallen to their knees and sung my praises, pinned me down and trembled with need.

All for *me*.

I sat back on my heels and wiped my hand across my mouth. "I wanna watch you two fuck each other."

He exhaled harshly. "Get up here and ride me, Flor. Show Paige how you like it."

With a coy grin, she crawled to him and swung her legs around his waist. His fingers grabbed at the metal he was tied to like he was trying to rip it apart. When she dropped her head towards his, Beau surged up and took her mouth and they groaned together. She kept them connected as she lowered herself onto his cock, and as his head fell back, she ran a tongue up the column of his throat.

They were so fucking beautiful together. And they were *mine*.

Flora planted her hands on his chest and fucked him in fast, short strokes. The sounds of their heavy breathing filled the room, and I watched her nails bite into his muscles. Watched her hips as she rose and fell, stared at the way her breasts shook, her nipples peaked, his lips half-curled in a snarl. They never took their eyes off each other, letting me in on a moment so private I felt decadently voyeuristic.

I grabbed the bottle of lube and coated my finger, fighting a smile when Beau saw and released a choked gasp. I cocked my head and waited for his permission.

"Fuck me while Flor rides me," he bit out. "Take me over the edge, gorgeous."

Flora sighed happily and moved faster, just as I pushed my finger inside him. His hips punched up at the invasion, and Flora squealed.

"Sweet *fucking Christ*," he cursed. "Don't stop."

I didn't, not even when she dropped her hands onto Beau's thighs and leaned back, putting her naked body on display right in front of me. I didn't pause to think. Instead, I bent my arm to keep my finger thrusting inside Beau and lowered my mouth to Flora's cunt. It took a few uncoordinated seconds to match her motions, but once I did, I lapped my tongue at her swollen clit.

She let out an agonized wail. Then she palmed the back of my head and held me there, grinding against my tongue with Beau's cock deep inside her. We were a mass of sweating, writhing bodies on the bed—hands and fingers and tongues, salt-slicked skin and their moans, rising in volume.

Flora came in huge spasms, rocking erratically against my mouth. Then she replanted her hands and rode Beau fast, slamming her hips down over and over. I twisted my finger inside him and matched her pace, until he came with a shout that shook the bed. She tumbled off a second later, and they lay together, breathing like they'd run ten miles through the snow.

I watched them with an affection so strong it threatened to crack my heart wide open.

He pressed a kiss to her forehead. "Are you okay?"

She laughed, reaching up to untie his wrists. "Never been better. How about you?"

"Feels like every single cell in my body got rearranged, but I'll manage." Then he crooked a finger my way. "Come here."

I moved toward them, almost shy after what we'd done. Beau gripped the back of my neck and pulled me close, giving me a bruising kiss. "That was like nothing I've ever felt before, ever experienced before. I could feel everything between us." His throat bobbed as he swallowed. "I could feel you and Flor, loving me."

She snuggled against his side. "You deserve all that love, Beau Duvall."

He stroked her hair. "So do you, darlin'."

When two sets of eyes landed on me, on my body, I felt the air shift from sleepy satisfaction to something darker. Hungrier.

Beau's hand on my neck closed around my throat. "We want you to feel how much we love you. Can we show you?"

"Yes," I whispered.

"Do you trust us?"

"Always."

His fingers tightened. "Go lay on your side by Flora."

I obeyed eagerly and was suddenly surrounded by them both—Flora in front of me, Beau curving around me from behind. Their bodies were so warm, an intriguing blend of solid and soft, and their fingers tangled together as they trailed their hands up and down, exploring.

She hooked two fingers inside of me as Beau palmed my aching breasts.

"Look at how beautifully you fit between us," she murmured. "Like you were always here, always with us."

He lifted the hair from my neck and roamed his mouth over the nape. While Flora sucked my nipple between her lips, he ground his cock against my ass. I cried out, already painfully close.

"We used to fantasize about you when we were in bed

together," Beau said roughly. "Talk about how we'd fuck you, what filthy things we'd do to this beautiful body."

I hummed under my breath. "Like what?"

There was a shifting on the bed—Flora and Beau moving downward. Two hot mouths, dancing along my rib cage, my shoulder blades, my spine, and my belly. I shivered from the dual sensations, from every teasing touch and wet tongue. She hooked my left leg onto her shoulder, curling her arm around to hold me open so she could give my pussy a long lick.

I gasped and looked down, her eyes locked on me as her tongue darted out again. I palmed her head, my fingers in her hair, and her eyes closed in pleasure.

Behind me, Beau was still trailing kisses down the entire length of my spine. His hands slid down my waist and gripped my ass cheeks, hefting and grabbing my flesh. A husky, appreciative sound rumbled from his chest while he closed his teeth around my skin.

"What I want to do to you here," he growled, biting me again. "We dreamed about this too, Paige."

"Wh-what?" I gasped. My lower body was trapped between them and being skillfully devoured by their mouths.

His thumb circled the tight ring of my ass. I clenched as another wave of pleasure washed over me. "Can I lick you here?"

"Yes, yes, please," I sobbed.

Beau's arm entwined with Flora's to prop up my leg. When I craned my neck to peek, my vision almost went dark at the seductive fantasy in front of me. Flora's face buried in my cunt and Beau's buried in my ass. I felt his breath feather over my sensitive skin and then his tongue, licking a smooth circle. His moved slow, maddeningly so, while Flora's darted fast.

I wasn't sure I could handle this much pleasure, this much sheer, overwhelming euphoria.

"Oh god, oh god, oh my god," I cried, growing incoherent the longer they lapped at me. He squeezed my ass as her tongue worked from side to side, sending me higher and higher and higher.

"I'm going to...I'm so..."

They increased the pressure of their mouths at the same exact time. It sent me soaring into a dazzling stratosphere I never wanted to return from. I came and came and came, writhing between them as they wrenched every last bit of pleasure from my body. I was trembling from head to toe, my chest heaving as I gasped. Flora stayed where she was, kissing my thighs, my hips. But Beau was crawling up my back and lining his cock against my entrance.

I hissed and arched, sensitive and needing to be fucked more than I needed oxygen to breathe. His right hand gripped my hip, fingers tight on my skin, and he ran his tongue up the back of my neck.

"I need to fuck you again," he groaned into my hair. "Just like this, with Flora's mouth on your cunt."

My mind went blank, every single thought vacating as I attempted to comprehend what that meant. A helpless keening came from the back of my throat. I reached behind and grabbed the back of Beau's head.

"Please, *now*."

He thrust his cock all the way inside, so deep that I cried out. Then he set a steady rhythm, rocking us in the sweetest grind. His cock dragged across every nerve ending—skillfully, deliberately. And his mouth stayed at my ear, so I could hear every rasping breath, every time he whispered my name.

Flora moaned from between my legs. I watched her dark eyes flick across our moving bodies, her fingers digging into the flesh of my hips. Her tongue moved in time with Beau's cock, firm, sweeping circles that made me wail and squirm.

And I thought I was soaring through a stratosphere before. This pleasure was indescribable, an unrelenting arc of ecstasy flowing across every nerve ending. I bucked against her mouth and pushed back on Beau's cock. Seeking both, needing both, overcome with how turned on they were.

Touching me, fucking me, loving me.

He slammed harder against me. "This is one of our favorite fantasies," he drawled in my ear. "Pinning you between us and fucking you without mercy, making you come so many times you beg us to stop."

"I wouldn't beg," I sighed. "I can take it all."

He twisted his hips and hit an angle that dimmed my vision. "That's right you can. You can, and you will."

Flora sucked my clit between her lips. I was balanced on the razor-thin edge of climax and losing my coherence.

"Come...come with me, Beau? Pl...please?"

He swore and bit my neck, working his cock between my legs as Flora flattened her tongue against my clit. This climax tore through me like a torrential rainstorm, brutal and savage and fierce. Destroying everything in my life I'd once known. Beau came with the same intensity, groaning my name and Flora's and losing himself in the final throes. I could feel him shuddering, could feel his panting breath against my nape.

And when he gently, tenderly, rolled away from me, he brought me to my back and peppered my temple and hair with kisses. I flopped my arms overhead, fully out of breath and still floating somewhere with the planets. Flora crawled up my body and cracked a cute smile.

"So was that okay?" she asked playfully.

"I'll never recover," I promised. "Leave me in this bed. I live here now."

"And did you feel us?" she asked, tracing my cheek with her finger. "Did you feel us loving you?"

It was like a fist closing around my throat. I heard all that was unsaid in those words—*you can trust us, you can love us, we want you forever*. I nodded, unable to speak, and her smile only grew more brilliant. Beau stroked my hair softly, and I closed my eyes, letting them soothe me as my head still spun.

"Flora," he said suddenly, amusement in his voice, "tell us what you need right now."

My eyes flew open again to find Flora writhing and chewing on her bottom lip. "I need to come after watching you."

Beau draped his arm over my waist, reaching for her. He twirled a finger, and she laid flat, legs wide. When his two fingers landed on her clit, her spine arched off the bed.

"Oh god, that's it," she chanted. "I'm already so close."

He worked his fingers and whispered at my ear. "Have you ever seen anything so beautiful? Look at her, Paige. She's a fucking angel. *Our* angel."

I curled onto my side and drank her in—her smooth belly, the red flush creeping up her neck, her honey-blond hair fanned out on the pillow. I took her nipple between my lips. She hissed and cupped my head, holding me there. I groaned, lapping at the tip as Beau circled her clit. Her skin was so soft, and the air smelled like our combined arousal. Sweat and salt and musk.

Flora came with a sharp, pleading cry then collapsed back against the bed with a sleepy smile.

Beau pulled us close, until we were nothing but a pile of tangled, exhausted limbs. Loved, on both sides.

Held and cherished and protected.

14

ALMOST MIDNIGHT

AFTER A MUCH-NEEDED NAP, THE THREE OF US GOT READY FOR our New Year's Eve dinner. It was already close to nine, the infamous countdown to midnight looming close. Flora cranked up the volume on a dance mix, then began prepping the food. The cabin slowly filled with the smells of baking bread and sizzling onions, which was only improved by the sounds of Flora, singing along to her favorite songs.

Meanwhile, my wet post-shower hair had dried into a snarled nest of tangles, so I hopped in the shower to wash it again. As the hot water cascaded down my skin, I took note of the bites and bruises, my slightly aching back, and the delicious burn between my legs.

I had so much to ask them. So much to worry about, once reality set in. And while the questions were many, the overall theme was: *how do we do this, and what if we break up and ruin everything in our life that was good?*

Still, my stomach flipped like a gymnast when Beau and Flora clapped and cheered for my New Year's Eve outfit in the kitchen. I came out to their wolf whistles and twirled beneath the tiny disco ball Beau had hung in the doorway.

He looked absurdly handsome in an aquamarine suit over a plain white tee, the sleeves of his jacket pushed up to show off the ink on his forearms.

Flora had donned a sparkly magenta minidress and a rhinestone tiara shaped like stars. And I was decked out in a long, sequin-covered blazer, with a lace crop top beneath and high-waisted trouser pants. Angel that she was, Flora had packed multiple choices for this weekend's celebration and let me shop her suitcase for the right outfit.

Beau did a sexy half-turn in his dress shoes. He'd brushed a pale, shimmery glitter across his cheekbones which only highlighted the intensity of his green eyes. "It's official. This is the hottest and queerest we've ever looked."

"You might be right." I grabbed him by the lapels and made a show of examining him from head to toe. "Though it's close. Clothing-wise, I slightly prefer you naked and tied to our bed."

He hooked his finger beneath my chin, tilting up so he could kiss me. "You know I can't wait to marry you, right?"

A smile burst across my face, and he matched it.

Flora appeared next to us. She clicked her tongue and tipped my face her way. "You smeared Paige's lipstick."

"Worth it," he called over his shoulder, moving to open a bottle of champagne.

"Give me the lipstick you always keep in your pocket," Flora said, palm open.

I rolled my eyes and complied. "It's not *always* there."

"Yes, it is. And you've been wearing this shade the entire time I've known you." She twisted it up and peeked at the bottom. "*Rogue Runaway.* I knew it. Every time I watched you apply this, I would get a little horny."

I pursed my lips and tried not to laugh. "Stop being so adorable, Flora. I cannot fucking handle it."

She gripped my chin and arched a dramatic brow. "*Shhh.* Let me live out this fantasy."

Our eyes met as she dragged the lipstick along my bottom lip. Her smooth skin shimmered against the magenta of her dress. Pale glitter highlighted the curve of her cheekbones beneath the disco ball, and her hair was loose and wavy. I wanted to bury my face in it, strip her out of this dress, and bend her right over the kitchen table.

Her brow lifted higher. "Are you thinking filthy thoughts about me, Paige Presley?"

"I've always been a sucker for a pretty girl in a minidress."

She angled my head side to side, assessing her work. "And I've always been a sucker for a pretty girl in a blazer." She rolled the tube back down, and I popped my lips together. "That's much better. You're officially New Year's Eve-worthy."

I took her hand in mine. "Here's to new and enchanting possibilities."

Beau appeared behind me, squeezing my shoulders. "Like finally telling our best friend that we're madly in love with her?"

Flora laughed, a bright and luminous sound. I bit the tip of my thumb, still completely baffled that they were talking about me.

"This weekend being New Year's Eve was especially fortuitous," she replied, shooting me a look of pure affection. The kind of look she regularly gave to Beau, an expression that said *I love you and I like you, a whole hell of a lot.*

I followed them to the high-top table, now pulled up to the floor-to-ceiling window that looked out upon the snowy wilderness. The flickering Christmas tree was reflected in the panes, as was the fireplace and the tiny, dazzling disco ball. A trio of candles sat in the middle of the table, surrounded by the meal that Flora had so lovingly prepared for us. A homemade pizza with the perfect amount of grease. A cutting board of cheeses with drizzled honey and almonds. A green salad, and a loaf of crispy bread.

Our glasses were refilled with fizzy champagne, and when we sat down together, our knees touching beneath the table, my worries about our future softened yet again. This moment—tender and flirty and comfortable—was one of a million moments between the three of us since we'd met, comprising the very foundation of our love. At first denied and forbidden, and now something I desperately wanted to fight for.

Almost immediately, our hunger took over, all of us starved after our day of hot sex and sledding in the cold. And as we ate, we reminisced about the many holidays we'd spent as friends since we met. The Christmases in cabins like this one. The boozy Pride parades followed by nights out dancing. Birthday camping trips and summer vacations spent kayaking down crisp, rushing rivers.

We shared shy smiles across the table, bejeweled in our New Year's Eve finest. They were everything I ever wanted. I just had to be brave enough to reach out and take it.

"The storm's passed, and we'll be leaving this weekend paradise soon," I said, drumming my nails against my glass. "And I want this to work between us, I really do. But I still have plenty of questions and worries, and I was hoping we could talk about them."

Beau released a shaky breath and nodded over at Flora. "We've got our own list of worries, but maybe you could go first? I'd love to hear what you're thinkin'."

I took a long sip of champagne before setting it down. "There's a lot of them. But I..." I swallowed hard. "I want the three of us together, committed and monogamous, if that continues to work for us. I want it to be equal, and I want us to love each other as passionately as we do now...but in public. Out to our community and our families. Is that what you want?"

Beau gave a crooked grin. "That's all we want. I'll tell the whole world as soon as we can. My sister already knows how we feel."

"Wait, you told Lily?" I asked, surprised.

"She was visiting us a few months ago. Got a little too drunk on tequila shots and *yelled* at me and Flora, asking when we were finally gonna make an honest woman out of you."

"She said that...*out loud*?"

He passed a hand over his jaw, still smiling. "It just about stunned us stupid. Made us wonder how obvious we'd been about our feelings whenever you were around. My parents are another story, but they adore you, Paige. Getting them to know what this is will be a huge hurdle. I'm not afraid of it though. Coming out as bi to them when I was sixteen wasn't easy either, but they approached it with open minds and have gone to more Pride parades than I have. What I want is for them to see that being in love with you has nothing to do with loving Flora *less*."

Flora took Beau's hand and squeezed. "My mom might be easier, since my sister is poly and often brings her partners over to Mom's house for dinner. She might not understand it, it might take time, but she knows there are people who love more than one person."

I propped my chin in my palm and stared at the flickering candles. "I'm ready to tell my dads...though I'm nervous, so if you want to be there with me, I'd appreciate it."

"Of course," she said.

"They think the world of you both, and I've been wondering, lately, if they've suspected something else going on. In some ways, they might not be surprised. But it'll still take some getting used to." I raised my gaze to study them both. "Do you think we'll get jealous?"

"Definitely," Flora said as Beau nodded emphatically. "I think we'll get jealous and have conflict and be in shitty moods sometimes. We've seen each other grumpy and exhausted and overwhelmed as friends. This will be no different. We'll need to set boundaries and communicate, go through all the growing pains of a new relationship. But it'll be more fun to argue with Beau about how he folds our laundry if you're there, Paige."

"Let the record show, I fold it the correct way," he said, index finger raised.

"It's the wrong way," she mouthed.

He laughed and dragged her to his chest as she squealed. "Paige will be our deciding vote."

I shrugged. "Who says I even fold my clothes? I believe in full-on laundry anarchy."

"*Oh no,*" Flora wailed.

Beau grinned wolfishly. "Oh, I can't wait."

I chewed over my next wish, finally opting to listen to my instincts instead of the squeaky fears in my brain. Fears that I understood were normal, no matter how much I loved them.

But my instincts were very, very clear.

"I want us to live together, just like this," I said. "Preferably if we could find a new place. Something we make and decorate as our own."

Flora cocked her head to one side. "Are you asking us to move into a big, happy house with you?"

"Yes," I said firmly. "Maybe not right away, but also...I wouldn't say no to doing it soon."

"So, like, does tomorrow work for you?" Beau asked, lips twitching.

I threw my napkin at his face. "You got it bad."

"I really, really do," he said, clutching his chest. "I'm an impatient man, and I want what I want. And that's to love the hell out of you both in as many ways as I can."

I couldn't stop the cheesy smile that spread across my face. Or the way my heart glowed when they leaned over to kiss me on the cheek.

"Beau captured my thoughts exactly," Flora said softly. "I'm ready for our love, no matter how messy."

"Are you afraid of anything though?" I asked. "Because I am."

His face darkened. "I'm afraid of a lot. Mostly that you'll leave us and we'll never recover, that we'll always be heartbroken."

Those words landed heavily between the three of us.

Flora nodded and said, "That's my fear. That for whatever reason, you won't love us back, and once you leave, our friendship *and* our relationship will be ruined."

"A situation like this has a lot of unique challenges," I said. "We'll need to communicate often and trust each other and even rebuild how to interact. I believe we *can* do that, and I'm ready to give it my all, but there's no sense in pretending as if it's always going to be easy."

Beau shook his head. "It won't always be easy. But it'll always be worth the risks we took to get there."

An anxious breath rushed from my lungs. "My biggest fear is that you'll leave me...but stay together. I know how close we are and how much our friendship has shaped me over the years. But I'm still the one coming into an already existing relationship. The power dynamic is there, even if we don't want it to be. And because of Em and Dorothy, it's hard for me to trust that I won't be abandoned again. When they left me for each other..." I trailed off, the emotions clogging my already tight throat. "I, uh...well, I don't ever want to feel so small and easily disposable ever again."

Beau cupped my face, his expression turning serious. "Then Flora and I will need to continue earning your trust to keep you. We're less without you, Paige. You're what's been missing all along, and whatever we need to do to even out that dynamic, we'll do, okay?"

"Okay," I said, already feeling a bit lighter having spoken the words out loud. "I'm not sure we can do much in the way of promises when it comes to things like this. We can't predict the future or how we'll grow and change. But I can say confidently that this feels right and natural and so beautiful already. I haven't felt this at *ease* in a long time, and I'm pretty sure it's because I'm not spending all this energy fighting my feelings for you. I want to fight for our love instead."

Flora stood and wrapped her arms around me from behind. Beau kissed my forehead, pulling us to his chest.

"Then let's fight for our love," he echoed.

"And I might have an idea that could help," Flora said.

15

WITH THIS RING

FLORA PULLED BEAU AND ME OVER TO THE CHRISTMAS TREE, the backs of our legs warmed by the fire crackling behind us. My breath caught at the look on her face—half nerves, half hope. And her eyes were shining as she gripped my hand in hers.

"You've planned so many weddings, Paige," she said, "so I want you to close your eyes and imagine what our wedding might look like. What it feels like, what it sounds like, the things that would make you happy. Can you do that?"

I laughed nervously but complied, feeling wings beating deep in my belly. My planning brain took over, sweeping along details and scenarios from past ceremonies that I loved, tossing the ideas that I loathed.

Until I recalled that those day-of details had never been important to me. Not when the most vital and precious thing in my life was the two people standing right here.

"This is a little blasphemous to say, given that I *am* a wedding planner," I started, "but I never fantasized about any of the things I help people make decisions about every day. Never cared about flowers or seating arrangements or what I would wear. I only ever pictured...community. A day celebrating queer love, what it means to carve out space for yourself in a world that wants to keep you invisible. Embracing a love that's beyond limits, as fresh and new as a sunrise. And I always wanted to be marrying the two of you."

A great surge of emotion had me fluttering open my eyes and blinking back tears. Beau's smile was larger than the Christmas tree we were standing next to.

And Flora was holding a ring in her hand. Her fingers trembled as they clasped mine. "Paige, I love your strength and your courage. I love how beautifully you give yourself to others, even if that means helping me at my bakery at four in the morning. I love how you start dancing as soon as we summit a hiking trail, how eagerly you chase adventure, how safe and protected you've always made me feel. And *yes*, I live for those red lips of yours and always will."

I was no longer in my body but floating above it, watching the woman of my dreams place a silver ring at the very tip of my finger.

"I'm head over heels in love with you. Will you marry me?" she asked.

Even with all that lay ahead of us, there was no hesitation and not an ounce of worry.

I knew what I wanted, knew what I deserved.

I always had.

"Yes," I blurted out. "Yes, *please*."

She beamed and kissed me, then carefully slid the ring onto my finger. Then she turned to Beau, now holding a second ring.

"Beau. I love that giant heart of yours and how wonderfully you give love to everyone around you. You make me laugh every single day, and I adore your compassion, your kind soul, your ability to comfort your patients when they need it. I'm so proud of every single thing you've accomplished, and I'm *really* proud of all the ways you've shown up for me in this relationship, even when we were confused and scared." She did the same thing, hovering the ring over his finger. "I love you with every fiber of my being. Will you marry me?"

He gripped her face. "Yes. And I'll say yes every time you ask."

On it went.

Next, Flora gave Beau two rings. They were mismatched and clearly ones she'd brought in her jewelry bag for the weekend, which only made it more intimate. The one I wore was still warm from her skin.

He cleared his throat and took my hand. When our eyes connected, I couldn't help but smile at his obvious nerves. "The day I realized I was in love with you, I wanted to run outside, shout to the world that what I felt was no fleeting crush, but something real and solid. That I loved every part of you—your brilliance, your confidence, your joy. All your nerdy movie tattoos, the way your hair shines in the moonlight. So I'm fully prepared to shout to the world how much I love you now, to anyone who'll listen, for as long as they let me."

I laughed, the back of my neck growing hot.

He took my hand and held out the ring. "I love you so much, Paige. Will you please, *please,* marry me?"

"I would be honored," I said, and he crushed me to his chest in a massive hug. The ring slid to the top of Flora's, and tears slid down my face.

When he twisted toward her, a gentle understanding swept over me. Of what she was trying to say, trying to show, about the true meaning of this specific gesture.

A brand-new start for three explorers, mapping their way to someplace singular and dazzling.

"Flor, I remember that road trip we took to Moab, when we watched the sunset together, and I felt this...this *weight* of love I'd never experienced before. I thought you were the most beautiful thing I'd ever seen, and I was so scared to tell you, so scared you'd turn me down. Instead, you taught me how to love better, how to *be* better. And I'd like to watch sunsets with you for the rest of my life. Will you marry me, darlin'?"

She pressed onto her toes and gave him a long kiss. "Yes," she whispered. "Always yes."

Then they faced me expectantly and Flora dropped the final two rings into the palm of my hand. I understood their significance as more than just a symbol but a promise. To live and love as boldly as we were able.

I swallowed a few times, a futile attempt to rein in my wild emotions. So I let everything show on my face—all my late-night worries, my secret desires, every fantasy and furtive wish.

I took Flora's hand in mine, admiring the ring she was already adorned with. "I love that you feed all the stray cats that live by the bakery and cook special treats for every dog that comes in. I love that your first instinct when a friend is in need is to bake them their favorite dessert, that every part of you comes alive in a kitchen where you practice your craft. On every hike, I forget my water bottle, and you always remember to bring it for me. You're the first to drag us someplace fun, the first to hug, the first to celebrate the small joys with your whole heart. I love you so much I can't imagine my life without you. Will you—" My voice broke. "Will you marry me?"

"Yes," she said, kissing me. "Yes, yes, a million times, yes."

She wiped the tears from my cheeks then allowed me to slip the second ring onto her hand.

I looked at Beau, and Flora stepped behind me and wrapped her arms around my waist. I took his hand, bolstered by the heat of her body curled around mine. He winked at me, as playful as ever, and it sent a burst of nervous laughter spilling from my lips.

"Beau, I love your spirit, how every day with you is as fun and silly as you are," I said. "I love how you're quick to come to the rescue, for your friends and for your patients. How your sense of wonder is boundless, and how appreciated you make people feel, just by being themselves. I love that your first question to me is usually if we should get a tattoo. You're always there to make me laugh, always there to tease, to show me how to reach for what I deserve. I love you, Beau, and I would be absolutely overjoyed if you married me."

His jaw ticked, his eyes shining in the glow of the holiday lights. "I would love to marry you, Paige Presley."

He immediately brought us close, wrapping his long arms around us as we laughed and cried. The weight of those rings on my fingers was effervescent, no heavier than the bubbles in our champagne glass.

It was the strength of Beau and Flora, holding me tight, that grounded me in that moment. The three of us. Together and ready to fight for each other.

The clock over the mantle chimed.

"Well, would you look at that," Flora said softly. "It's midnight. Happy New Year, my darlings. We made it."

16

A BOUNDLESS JOY

WE ENDED UP BACK IN THAT GIANT BED OUT OF A FIERCE, driving necessity. Stripped down to nothing but our new rings, Beau pinned Flora's arms as I balanced over her with a glass of champagne in my hand.

"Engagements need to be celebrated," I murmured, dribbling a splash onto her belly. She hissed, hips writhing, and I watched as golden droplets slid along her skin. Another splash between her breasts, and a third into the hollow of her throat. "How do you think we should do that, Beau?"

He dipped his mouth down her collarbone and ran his tongue through the liquid. "I have some ideas."

"Really? Because so do I."

I gripped Flora's hips and held her still, catching the drops with my tongue. Sucking her sweetened, sticky skin between my lips and using my teeth to mark her. My hands collided with Beau's as we roamed her gorgeous body, our mouths meeting in rough kisses. She reared up and dragged me down, thrusting against me while I licked her throat. Beau was next to us, on top of us, the three of us a blur of limbs and sighs.

His fingers slid between her legs, and I fisted his cock, stroking up until he groaned. They panted together, arching into me, and I basked in the heady realization that these two people were now mine forever. To love and tease and kiss and fuck.

This time was less coordinated, our actions borne of the passionate vows we'd just made to each other. Beau ran his tongue between my breasts. Flora sucked his cock, slow and deep. His talented fingers curled inside me, making my eyes roll back when he slid against my G-spot. Her tongue danced across my clit, and I sucked her nipples into my mouth. His lips landed hot and heavy on mine, his grip hard around my chin.

We built into a fever pitch in the middle of that bed as fireworks burst in the sky. There was no natural end to our desire, no limit to what we were willing to do for each other. I tasted every drop of sweat and champagne on Flora's body. Took Beau's shaft into my mouth and reveled in his shuddered breath. Lost my mind when they licked my nipples together, stringing me so tight I almost came.

Flora shoved Beau backward onto the bed and tightened her hand around his throat. With a smug look, she straddled his thighs and lowered herself onto his cock.

He grabbed her hips with a growl. "Is that what you need? To fuck me into oblivion?"

She crooked a finger at me and pointed to his face. "I need Paige to ride your mouth while I ride your cock. And you don't come until we say you can."

His grin flashed. "Yes, ma'am, I swear it."

Flora planted her hands and started to grind, her head falling back as soon as she moved. I crawled toward the top of the bed and Beau's sinful mouth.

"That's it, Flor," he bit out. "*Fuck,* that's so good. Paige...*shit*...I need that sweet cunt on my tongue."

With a sly smile, I swung my legs over his face. His chest rumbled with satisfaction, and he grabbed my ass with one hand, flattening his tongue so I could rock against it.

I gasped out an, "*Oh thank god,*" and then Flora was kissing me. She moved up and down on his cock, and I did the same on his tongue, and we were one graceful motion together.

"I'm so close already," I sobbed against her. Beau gave me a teasing smack on my ass and fluttered his tongue faster. "*Yes, Beau.* So good, so good, so good."

She gripped my face with one hand and began circling her clit with the other. "Come with me, Paige. I'm right there with you."

She captured my lips, and we groaned together. I felt him thrusting up from the bed. His tongue had me balanced on the edge, but then he sucked my clit between his lips and I flew over. Flora and I came, bucking and writhing on top of Beau, every nerve ending in my body alight.

She very, *very* carefully lifted herself from his cock. He was still hard as steel, slick and veined. I tumbled from Beau's face and grinned at his expression, some combination of tortured and ecstatic.

"You wanna tie me down and use me like that again?" he drawled. "Say the word, and I'm yours."

"That's good to know," I panted, dragging a finger up his length. He jumped and shuddered. Flora gave his hair a sharp tug. "Did you come?"

"No, ma'am."

"Good. Now fuck Paige on her hands and knees."

He reared up, hovered his mouth over hers. "Like how I

fucked you last night? When Paige listened to us through the wall?"

"Just like that," she said. "And I love tasting her on you."

My fingers were already curling into the sheets, my core clenching. Beau's eyes slid to mine, and the fire there scorched through every inch of my body. "Is that what you want, Paige?"

"Yes," I panted.

He traced a line down Flora's throat. "And where will you be?"

With a seductive smile, she crawled across the bed and sat in front of me, knees together. She spread them, exposing her glistening pussy. I dropped my face and pressed it between her thighs, breathing her in.

"I'll be right here," she said, sifting her fingers through my curls.

I took a long, greedy swipe. "I love this. I love *you.*"

"I know you do," she murmured. She lay back with her arms overhead, back lifting as I teased my tongue through her. The bed dipped behind me. Beau's lips landed on my spine, tracing a hot path downward.

"So beautiful," he said. "Both of you. And so sexy I feel like I'm dreamin'."

I circled her clit and shivered at his words. Then his hands gripped my waist. I arched shamelessly and heard him chuckle. He gave me another smack and then he was thrusting inside me. The invasion sparked to life every orgasmic aftershock, sending me wailing into her pussy.

"Holy shit, you feel incredible," he groaned. His pace was unrelenting, his cock driving fast and deep and so thoroughly I lost all ability to think. My tongue moved on Flora, who was writhing and perfect in front of me. She chanted my name and he growled it and I was trapped between them both. Fucked and used, taken and taking, our mutual pleasure in a perpetual cycle.

"Beau," Flora begged, "I want you to come. Need to... need to see you now. Both of you together, in front of me like this...*oh my god.*"

I dug my fingers into her thighs and sped up my movements. Panted "oh fuck" when Beau bore down between my legs. Two of his fingers landed on my clit and circled. My tongue faltered, pleasure crashing through me, taking me higher.

Flora grabbed my face, grinding into my mouth. She was the first of us to come, screaming my name and thrashing. I only had a second to flash her a smug smile before my own climax ripped through me. I clamped down so hard around Beau's cock that he cursed.

"Goddammit, Paige, *fuck,*" he said. I pressed my face to the mattress and moaned through the rest of it, loving how out of control he felt behind me. His orgasm seemed to last forever, wringing everything out of him.

When he collapsed in a heap next to us, I started to laugh, a combination of emotional exhaustion and physical elation. Beau joined in after me, followed by Flora, until tears rolled down our cheeks.

It was as much a release as everything else we'd done.

We spooned against each other as the sweat dried on our skin and our breathing returned to normal. Beau scratched his fingers through my hair, and I did the same to Flora.

So much contentment settled over me it was almost scary, but I recognized it for what it really was. Freedom. Authenticity. The candy-sweet ache of liberation from everything we believed was holding us back.

"I might be coming around to this New Year's thing," Beau said.

"Told ya," Flora teased. "It's the best holiday there is. Glitter, countdowns, dance parties—"

"Group sex," I added.

Laughter rumbled from his chest. "It's the reason for the season."

The fireworks outside continued to light up the sky, bathing our bodies in blues and reds and vibrant purples. Refracting off the silver and gold bands of our rings, over and over again.

Sleep wasn't a priority that night, though we managed to find it in fits and starts. In between, we reached for each other. Moving together, fucking and kissing and tasting every inch. Shuddering through orgasm after orgasm until Beau and Flora fell into a restless sleep close to dawn.

I stayed awake though, eager to watch the wintry sunrise I'd longed for since we arrived.

The roads would open soon, our weekend respite ending as the temperatures rose and the ice melted. But at dawn, the snow outside was still powdery fresh and new. Fingers of daylight slipped through the pine trees surrounding us, and distant bird songs chirped through the narrow valley.

The sky outside shifted, from dark indigo to pale pink to a muted coral.

Beau was curled up with his head on my chest, and Flora was snuggled into my side. I gazed down at these two people I loved, safe in my arms even as we were ready to meet whatever came next.

Our love was infinite, our joy boundless.

As vast as that sunrise and brimming over with magic.

EPILOGUE
ONE YEAR LATER

WE WERE BACK AT THE SKI LODGE IN TELLURIDE, ONLY THIS time the wedding was a sure thing.

Flora was still red-cheeked and slightly out of breath as she re-knotted Beau's tie. I brushed a hand down her long lace gown then made sure no bite marks were visible on my throat. Dusted off a stray thread on my white pantsuit and slipped back into my heels.

Beau wore a lopsided grin while he tightened his cuff links. "I told ya we could be fast."

I snorted as I fixed my smudged lipstick in the mirror. "I knew we'd be in trouble if we came up to change together."

"Is that a complaint I hear?" He nuzzled my nape. "'Cause I believe you were calling *both* our names not three minutes ago."

I fought a smile as he met my gaze. "No complaints, just stating a fact. You've always been trouble, Beau Duvall."

"Tell me about it," Flora teased. She turned and let me adjust her very pretty, very delicate crown of daisies. "The man's obsessed with us."

He gave her a smacking kiss on the cheek, and she

laughed. "I'm about to marry my beautiful soulmates. *Obsessed* ain't half of it."

I re-pinned his boutonniere and admired the look of my wedding rings against his black tuxedo. After some resizing, we'd kept the ones Flora had given us that night, and the memory was such a sweet one I was blinking back tears.

"Hey," Beau said softly, "you okay, gorgeous?"

I pressed the edge of my palm beneath my eye. "I'm thinking about us at that cabin a year ago, proposing to each other on New Year's Eve. How I never knew I could be this happy. Even thought for a while that I didn't deserve it. And now...*this*. Everyone we love, downstairs, dancing their faces off beneath a ceiling filled with disco balls."

Flora wrapped her arms around my waist and kissed my hair. "They don't even know the surprise yet."

I touched my wrist. We'd gotten matching tattoos a few months ago—a small, simple mountain range with the sun rising behind it. To represent our weekend in that cabin and all that we'd learned there. This past year together was not without its ups and downs. We had some family members who took longer to support our relationship than others. Had our own challenges as we navigated an entirely new relationship, one none of us had ever been in before. We discovered patience and flexibility, and most of all, we kept trust at the center of all of it.

In the end, Flora *did* win the laundry argument. Though Beau retaliated by tossing her, laughing, onto the bed and demanding that he and I pay penance for all the socks we'd folded incorrectly.

In the months after we came back, I began planning more weddings for clients whose relationships looked like mine. I'd done four so far, and the people I'd met had offered us so much advice, broadening our community so we always had someone to turn to when we had questions. I'd also planned three coming out parties, one adoption celebration, and a handful of "just because" parties. For those warm Tuesdays in October just because the leaves are changing. Fridays in the springtime when the air finally turns balmy after the long winter. Saturday nights in the summer when the sun never sets and the days feel endless.

After risking so much to be together, we embraced our days with a reckless abandon that made my heart sing. Our friendship grew stronger, our passion grew hotter, our love was as expansive as the sky above.

Beau took a breath and rubbed his palms together. "Speaking of...are we ready?"

Flora nodded, taking my hand and then his. "Let's go declare our big queer love for the world to see."

And then I let my soulmates lead me out into a dance party that was truly going full swing. We'd rented the same lodge we'd visited a year ago, telling our friends and family we were throwing a one-year-anniversary bash. It was disco-themed, so everyone showed up in head-to-toe glitter and platform shoes, twirling around in colorful dresses and bell bottoms. When it became obvious that people were noticing us standing on a small platform in wedding attire, we had the DJ cut the music.

My dads turned and saw me—dapper white suit and all —and their expressions of happy, tearful surprise had my heart skipping in my chest.

But then Flora handed me the mic, and that same heart rejoiced in anticipation.

I cleared my throat as the crowd quieted. "You might have guessed by our sudden outfit changes that we convinced you all to celebrate New Year's Eve here under false pretenses. In about five minutes or so, you'll be guests at our wedding."

There came a chorus of shocked laughter, a smattering of cheers and applause, some delighted gasps.

"But before that, we wanted to thank all of you for showing us what community really means these past twelve months. We asked you to support our relationship, and you did more than that—you encouraged it, celebrated it, seemed genuinely overjoyed to see us finally together."

Flora took my hand while Beau looped an arm around my shoulders.

"You fought for us the way we fought for each other. And nothing's more queer than that—purposefully taking up space, demanding to be seen, shining forward in every way possible." My voice caught. "We owe everything...*everything* to the people in this room. You taught us an abundance of imagination, you gave us pride, you allowed us to pursue an enchanting new possibility. And you never once stopped and asked 'but why?' You always said 'why *not*?' Why not reach for joy, in big heaping handfuls, until you're filled to the brim with it?"

Tears tracked down my cheeks. Beau brushed a kiss across my temple, and Flora wrapped her arms around my waist.

"The symbols of this ceremony mean nothing without the people behind it. And that's all of you," I said. "Thank you for believing in our love."

I looked at Beau and Flora, gorgeous and dazzling beneath the disco light.

"Let's get married, shall we?"

THE END

BONUS EPILOGUE

Thirty minutes earlier

Our pre-wedding quickie was undeniable from the moment we stepped into our bedroom to change.

My body already shivered with a decadent blend of nerves and adrenaline. And the thrum of arousal from being around Beau and Flora all night was a constant state at this point. It didn't help that they seemed to be teasing me on *purpose*. Raspy whispers against my ear. A stray touch at my waist, the inside of my wrist. Flora's pretty eyes drinking me in. Beau's half-grin and secret winks.

But *still*. We were supposed to be surprising our friends and family with a spontaneous wedding in twenty-nine minutes. Giving in to temptation felt out of the question.

I shouldn't have been surprised when I stepped out of the closet, arms full of our wedding attire, to find Flora on her knees in front of Beau. His button-down shirt was open, tattooed muscles flexing, both hands buried in her golden hair.

She was barefoot, still in her minidress, though it

bunched at her waist, revealing her round ass. Her head bobbed as she sucked his cock deeper, and his rough groan weakened my knees. His eyes blazed with lust when they found mine from across the room.

His jaw ticked. "Lock that door, then get over here."

All the air left my lungs, my craving for them growing from a simmer to a wildfire in a matter of seconds. I gently placed our clothing on an armchair before checking the locked door, suddenly grateful for the loud, pulsing music beneath our feet.

It meant whatever we did next wouldn't be heard.

Beau crooked his finger, and I was at their side a moment later. My hand joined his on the back of Flora's head, and she moaned around his shaft. His other hand yanked me close for a ravenous kiss. I opened for him, felt his growling hunger, his barely leashed control.

I tipped my head back, sighing as he bit and licked down my throat. "We only...we only have twenty minutes. Maybe...maybe less."

His answering chuckle was dark and dangerous. "Getting you both off fast isn't a problem, gorgeous. Give me fifteen minutes, and you'll be thanking me all night."

His hand slipped between my legs, cupping my pussy with the perfect amount of pressure. I whimpered, managing to say, "Such an arrogant boyfriend."

"*Husband*," he said against my ear. "I'm your fucking husband, which means I'll get you off as fast as I'd like."

Behind me, Flora had risen from her knees and was working my pants down. Then she slid her hands beneath my tank and palmed my breasts. "That's something your wife can do too, you know," she teased. I turned my head, finding her lips, giving in to a long kiss.

"Oh, I know you can." I slipped a hand between her legs,

circling her clit. She melted into me, wrapping her arms around my neck while she whimpered against my mouth. "It's not a competition, though. You can *both* work at getting me off fast."

Beau nipped my ear. "Being a brat on your wedding day?"

I arched back, grinding my ass into his cock. He hissed and shuddered, biting me harder. Then giving Flora a bruising kiss, trapping me between them—my hand between her legs, his hips pushing forward.

"I want both of my wives on that bed," Beau demanded. "And keep that dress on, Flor. I wanna ruin you in it."

I kicked off my pants and tossed my shirt and bra. Flora spread out on the bed, looking debauched and gorgeous. Hair down, dress rucked up, her pussy naked and glistening. Beau fell to his knees and yanked her toward his face, inhaling with a pained groan. They were beautiful together —the muscles rippling between his shoulder blades, her fingers twisting in his hair, his tongue giving her clit long strokes.

I crawled onto the bed next to her and gave the top of her dress a rough tug. Her nipples hardened in my mouth as I sucked on them, both Beau and I feasting on every inch of her body. I turned my head, and my eyes met Beau's, staring avidly while his tongue danced over Flora's clit. A delicious thrill shot through me as he watched me lap at her breasts, timing my licks with his. His right arm bunched and flexed, and I knew the moment he thrust his fingers inside of her.

"Oh god oh god oh—" she started to chant. I crashed our lips together, swallowing her cries as her back arched up. She was just so *delicious* like this. Half-naked and panting and writhing between the two of us. When Beau smacked my ass, I knew what he wanted me to do. I gave Flora a grin then turned to face him just as he was adding a third finger, stretching her. He sat back on his heels and arched a brow, the command obvious.

So I dipped my head between her legs and sucked her clit between my lips. His one hand shot forward and covered Flora's mouth while we worked her over together—my tongue circling while he finger-fucked her in fast, rough strokes.

Her orgasm came a few seconds later, sending her hips bucking. Her squeals were barely muffled by Beau's palm.

"That's it, darlin'," he grunted. "You're so fucking beautiful when you come like this."

I was already so close I could taste it. Had to keep squeezing my thighs together as the sounds of Flora's climax slowly became soft whimpers, then relieved sighs. We fell onto her after that, Beau and I kissing up her neck, competing for her mouth.

"How much time do we have now?" I asked, nuzzling her hair.

Flora laughed softly as Beau's hot gaze shot to mine. "Don't you worry about that," he drawled. He reached forward, flipping me onto my back and then dragging me to the end of the bed. He pushed my knees wide, staring down at my cunt. "There's nothing more important than this moment right here." His eyes traveled the length of my body and then he cupped Flora's face. "Nothing more important to me than you two, your pleasure, your happiness. It could be ten minutes or ten years, I'll do anything to make you look at me the way you're both looking at me now."

"And how's that?" Flora asked.

He swallowed. "Like you love me more than anything else."

"That's because we do," I said, hooking my fingers with his.

His lips curved as he thrust every inch of his cock inside of me. My spine lifted off the bed as a strangled groan fell from my lips. "Oh *god,* and I love this too."

"Of course you fucking love this," he hissed, thrusting his hips forward. "We're perfect together, all three of us. Always have been."

Beau hitched my knees high, exposing me to his and Flora's movements. His cock filled me up just right, stretching and stroking and hitting *everything.* I watched his head tip back, the bob of his throat, his fingers tight on my skin.

Flora lowered herself down my body. And with Beau hard and unrelenting inside of me, she curled her tongue around my clit, and I opened my mouth to scream. Like before, his hand cupped my mouth, which only turned me on more. With my moans muffled, I could only watch Flora's tongue lap at my slick skin, could only watch Beau grind himself between my legs faster and faster.

After a year together, they knew how to play my body like a treasured instrument. It was how they made me feel, night after night—treasured and precious and debauched, all at once. A powerful orgasm sped through me like a train, and I screamed into Beau's palm. He followed me over the edge, growling our names with his final thrusts.

And as the three of us lay back on the bed—entwined and sweating and out of breath—I saw the clock on the wall nearing midnight. Knew it meant one singular and vital thing.

It was time for a surprise wedding.

ACKNOWLEDGMENTS

Thank you for reading my hot New Year's Eve novella about three bisexual friends who have been madly in love with each other this whole time! I had *so much fun* with this project. It's my first book where every main character is queer (specifically, they are disaster bisexuals like me!) and even though I've been pitching this story as something light and spicy (which it is), it's also meant so very much to me. It's a little scary to write with my whole, super-queer heart, but I'm grateful to be able to do so.

After my best friend read the first draft of this book, she said, "As soon as you tell me it's simply filthy, I know it's really about the power of undying love." She was right (as always). The idea to write a sexy fantasy about a wedding planner falling for the couple came screeching into my brain fully formed and wouldn't let me go. But of course, it actually became a story about imagining new possibilities for what love and commitment can really mean.

Here's to dismantling binaries, reaching for joy, and loving with reckless abandon!

And now, a giant, glitter-filled thank you to my community:

For my besties, who have always loved me just the way that I am (and it will not surprise you to learn that *none of us* can sit in a chair properly).

For my incredible editors and beta readers (Faith, Jodi, Julia, Bronwyn, Jessica and Emily) whose support, feedback and cheery notes thrilled me to no end. This novella wouldn't be the same without them.

Thank you, as always, to TWSS for alllllll the impressive work that goes into sending a book (even a little one like KEEP YOU BOTH) out into the world. And for Staci Hart, who designed the *perfect* cover. And to Joyce, Tammy, Lucy, Stephanie, LJ and Avery, who have all supported me so much during this very different year.

And to Rob, my real-life enchanting possibility— marrying you was the best decision I ever made.

HANG OUT WITH KATHRYN!

Sign up for my newsletter and receive exclusive content, bonus scenes and more!
I've got a reader group on Facebook called **Kathryn Nolan's Hippie Chicks.** We're all about motivation, girl power, sexy short stories and empowerment! Come join us.

Let's be friends on
Website: authorkathrynnolan.com
Instagram at: kathrynnolanromance
Facebook at: KatNolanRomance
Follow me on BookBub
Follow me on Amazon

ABOUT KATHRYN

Kathryn Nolan is an Amazon Top 25 bestselling author. Her steamy romance novels are known for their slow-burn sexual tension, memorable characters, and big, hopeful feelings.

Kathryn is a bisexual bookworm with big Leo energy. She loves to spend her free time hiking, camping and traveling in her camper van ("Van Morrison"). When not on the road, she lives in her hometown of Philly with her cute husband and giant-eared rescue pup, Walter.

Sign up for Kathryn's weekly newsletter to see what she's writing, what she's reading/watching and get all her travel stories (plus an abundance of Walter photos!):

https://www.authorkathrynnolan.com/join-my-newsletter

BOOKS BY KATHRYN